Alice in Neverland

AIRSHIP 27 PRODUCTIONS

™

"Alice in Neverland"
© 2020 R.A. Jones

Published by Airship 27 Productions
www.airship27.com
www.airship27hangar.com

Interior illustrations © 2020 Gary Kato
Cover illustration © 2020 Ted Hammond

Editor: Ron Fortier
Associate Editor: Fred Adams Jr.
Marketing and Promotions Manager: Michael Vance
Production designer: Rob Davis

ISBN: 978-1-946183-93-4

Printed in the United States of America

10 9 8 7 6 5 4 3 2 1

Alice in Neverland

R.A. Jones

Dedicated to those who are young...
And to those who are young at heart!

Map of Neverland

Chapter 1

Alice was a very proper young lady; no one could ever truthfully say otherwise.

At the moment, as she sat in the parlor of her family's home, she was dressed all in black. This was only appropriate, given the recent passing of both her parents.

The house was filled with people, mourners who had come to pay their respects following the dual memorial service.

Alice didn't know most of them. Still, she attempted to be cordial and polite to each and every one of them, as she thought would be expected of a proper young British woman.

So thoroughly did she maintain her composure, however, that some (who had nothing better to do) would later comment that the girl appeared to be totally aloof, as though unfeeling or uncaring.

As such people usually are, they were quite mistaken.

Inside, which is the only side that really matters, Alice was grieving most heartily. She had deeply loved her mother and father, and to have both of them snatched away from her so suddenly and so horribly by the dreaded cholera was almost more than Alice could bear.

But bear it she did, nodding and even occasionally smiling wanly at the well-wishers as they offered condolences, advice and opinions. None of which she really heard, of course.

And then, a blessed relief, at last they were all gone.

Or nearly all. Alice's older sister Elsbeth remained, along with Elsbeth's husband Aubrey. While the two of them sat together in the drawing room, Alice busied herself by helping the servants clean up and straighten up after all the well-meaning mourners.

The servants could have done it all quite well without the girl's assistance, of course. But they were ordinary people, and being ordinary made them less self-absorbed; so they knew Alice needed to keep busy and they respected that.

In the horrible aftermath of losing both parents within a day of one another, the girl had found it virtually impossible to sleep and she desperately needed to keep her mind and her body fully occupied during her waking hours lest she succumb to grief and shock.

She was feverishly dusting away at an already spotless end table when her sister laid a gently restraining hand on her arm to stop her.

"It's time we talked, Alice," Elsbeth said. Aubrey nodded in agreement. His agreeableness was perhaps the main reason Elsbeth had married him.

"About what?" Alice asked her sister.

"About the future."

"Already? I can barely grasp the present."

"That's what I'm here for, Alice. You'll learn soon enough that it's better to think about what hasn't happened yet than to dwell on what already has."

"What?" Somehow, that didn't totally make sense to Alice.

"Never mind. Here's what's important. Da and Ma left the estate in my hands. Aubrey and I have decided to sell the house."

"What?" Alice jerked as if being rudely shaken awake. "But—but where shall *I* live?"

"With *us*, you silly goose." Alice noticed that the nod Aubrey gave to this pronouncement seemed somewhat less enthusiastic.

"But I don't want to live anywhere else," Alice insisted. "This is the only home I've ever known."

"I know, dear Alice," Elsbeth said, reaching out to pat her sister on the knee.

"But you have no means of supporting yourself or of paying for the upkeep of a house. And even if you could—it wouldn't be proper for a young girl to live alone.

"And by living with Aubrey and me, you can also be properly groomed for the prospect of marriage."

"*Marriage*?" Alice exclaimed. "I haven't given that any thought at all!"

"Exactly my point. You simply *must* think about it, Alice. After all—you're not a child any more, you know. You'll soon be fifteen years old; you're not much younger than I was when Aubrey and I were wed."

Alice sighed heavily. "I can remember a time, Elsbeth, when you told me you hoped I would always keep the simple and loving heart of childhood."

"I'm afraid you've already lost that," Elsbeth replied much too brusquely. "And it might be well for you if you have!"

Alice's shoulders slumped in defeat. "When do you want me to move in with you?"

"Right now. At once. Come with us now."

"Oh, no! Not so soon—please!"

"When would you suggest, then?"

Alice's mind whirled as she tried to think clearly. "Tomorrow," she said at last. "Surely tomorrow will be soon enough. And that will give me one last night to spend here in the house before I have to tell it good-bye forever!"

Uncertain, Elsbeth glanced up at Aubrey, who gave her a short, curt nod. (Was nodding the only form of communication of which this man was capable, Alice wondered.)

"Very well," Elsbeth said, rising to her feet. "But first thing tomorrow morning, we're coming back for you."

And with that…Alice was left more alone than she had ever been in her life.

Chapter 2

Alice's father had given her a small allowance at the end of each week as a reward for her performing all her required household chores. She had diligently set aside a few pence of that allowance every month, saving it against future need.

She now used a small portion of her savings to avail herself of the services of a hansom cab. Following her instructions, the cab driver deposited her in the middle of London's Kensington Gardens.

Not wishing to draw undue attention to herself, Alice had changed out of her black mourning clothes and into a prim blue dress and white pinafore.

On many a pleasant Sunday afternoon, Alice and her parents had strolled the Gardens together and she now took great comfort in the old and arching trees that lined its walkways.

Constancy is often the source of comfort for people. A schedule that is followed strictly every day. A closet filled with identical changes of clothes. A diet that seldom varies. Institution and establishments that have always been here and will always remain. Familiar faces.

While some might be driven mad by the boredom of a non-altering life, others found peace and tranquility from knowing that today would be just like yesterday and that tomorrow would be identical to today. Understandably, Alice at the moment desperately wanted and needed… her yesterday.

Still, even in this warm and familiar setting, her mind was abuzz. So much had changed in such a short period of time. Her entire life, in fact. What lay ahead of her was hidden from her ability to imagine.

It also just did not seem right to the girl that all the people passing her on every side seemed to be going about their normal lives as if nothing had happened. Her parents were gone forever: why were these heartless people not just as shattered as she was?

(To think such thoughts, irrational though they may be, is common when one is grieving. It's hard to see beyond your own pain.)

More than once during the course of her leisurely stroll, Alice paused to look around her. If you have ever experienced that feeling that some-one somewhere is watching you, then you well know exactly how young Alice felt.

In a place filled with so many other people, people she didn't know, Alice couldn't tell if such was really the case, so she shrugged it off and continued her stroll.

The truth was, Alice *was* being watched.

Watched by someone who was in turn being watched by yet someone else!

Chapter 3

"Go to the attic, Alice."

Alice awoke with a start. After returning home to her now empty house and partaking of a supper that consisted of nothing more than biscuits and tea, Alice had allowed herself a luxury she had forefended for nearly a week.

She had cried.

She didn't care if this was childish of her; she didn't care if it was not proper. She cried for the loss of her parents and, yes, for the loss of the life that would no longer again be hers to enjoy. She cried until the wracking sobs caused her to cough and choke.

She cried because she needed to cry, as sometimes happens to us all.

And when the sobs subsided, she took herself to bed. As had been the case since the deaths of her mother and father, sleep did not come easily or quickly, but the fingers of sheer exhaustion did at last push her eyelids closed. It was a deep sleep, devoid of dreams.

Then the voice awakened her.

She lay in the dark, listening, but heard no further sound. Deciding that she had merely been dreaming, she rolled back onto her side.

"Go to the attic, Alice."

Now she had heard the words distinctly and knew she was not asleep, not dreaming.

Rising from her bed, Alice removed her nightgown and pulled on her dress, pinafore and shoes. Why she did this, she could not have said for sure.

Lighting a candle, she proceeded to slowly climb the stairs that led up to the attic of the house. Every few steps she would pause and listen, but the whispering voice did not return.

The hatch leading up into the attic creaked eerily as Alice cautiously poked her head and shoulders up and peered left and right. She had not been in the attic in years, but everything inside it looked as one would expect: mostly old chests and boxes and discarded furnishings covered by dusty sheets.

As she then walked about the attic, careful not to bump her head on low-lying rafter beams, the pale aura of light fluttering outward from the candle caused macabre shadows to rise up and dance around Alice on all sides.

Though the urgent, whispering voice spoke no more to her, still did Alice feel as if something was beckoning her to a far corner of the attic. A tall but thin object stood there, completely obscured beneath a sheet.

Holding the candle high in her left hand, Alice stretched her right hand toward the covering sheet. She stopped, holding her breath and pulling her hand back away.

Her slender fingers trembled slightly as she again reached for the sheet. When her hand touched the cool cloth, she clutched it and pulled it away with one sharp tug.

"*Ah!*" Alice cried—as she saw a *face* staring out at her!

Chapter 4

Alice fell backward onto the floorboards of the attic. She began to cough and sneeze as loosened clouds of dust swirled round about her. At the same time, she tried to crawl away from the shadowy face that had confronted her.

She thrust her blazing candle forward, as if hoping it would act as a talisman that would ward off any evil that might be preparing to launch itself upon her. She clenched her eyes shut and again sucked in her breath.

Nothing happened.

Silence once more descended upon the attic. No icy fingers from beyond reached out to grab her. Finally, Alice opened her eyes.

What she saw caused her to smile and lightly chide herself for being such a child.

The object she had uncovered was a *mirror*. And the "face" that had leered out at her—was merely her own reflection!

In the light from her candle, Alice took a moment or two to gaze at her own image. She had always worried that she had too plain a countenance, even though her mother, while brushing out her flaxen hair at night, often told her she was quite beautiful.

She knew that physical beauty should not be the only measure of a person's worth and that vanity was not a virtue. Still, she did always strive to look her very best.

Alice wasn't sure at the moment if anyone would find her pretty. Sorrow and grief have a way of draining even the glow of youth. One of her sorrows was the knowledge that her mother would never again brush her hair.

She sighed and gazed more thoroughly at the entire mirror.

Upon closer inspection, she recognized the large looking glass as being one that in an earlier time had decorated the top of the fireplace mantle in the downstairs' drawing room.

Seeing the looking glass caused Alice, for the first time in ages, to think back to one of the more vivid *dreams* she had experienced in her childhood.

In that dream, Alice had literally stepped *through* the mirror—emerging for the second time in that strange place called *Wonderland*.

Wonderland had been the queerest province imaginable—not surprising, Alice supposed, given that it was *completely* imaginary. It was inhabited by strange beasts, including a rabbit with a watch, a giant caterpillar and an enigmatic cat that could appear and disappear at will. The people there were equally odd and usually of a most disagreeable nature. It was a world in which the nonsensical was the norm and normalcy was nonsense. Being normal almost to the extreme, Alice of course found herself to be both utterly out of place yet strangely captivated by this domain of lunacy.

Elsbeth and her parents had all assured Alice that these almost magical journeys were indeed nothing more than products of her own, overly active imagination, gone wild and given vivid form while she was asleep.

It had always been a pleasure to awaken from these mostly frustrating nocturnal visits; yet there was a part of Alice—the more adventurous part—that was saddened when the dreams stopped coming to her.

Also, Alice now recalled, not long after she had "returned" from that second dream journey, her father had rather unceremoniously *removed* the looking glass from its perch atop the mantle. She now knew what had become of it.

Alice never gave it a second thought until tonight. Nor had she experienced another dream of traveling to Wonderland. Seven years and a little more had passed since that time: nearly half her brief life.

In a soft voice, barely above a whisper, Alice recited a line from a poem she had once read.

Life, what is it but a dream?

On impulse, Alice reached out to touch the looking glass. As her hand drew near to the mirror, its slightly fogged surface seemed almost to melt away, just like a bright, silvery mist.

Her eyes and mouth widened in wonderment as her hand did not stop at the surface of the mirror—but rather passed through it and out of sight!

Reflexes caused her to snatch her hand and arm back out of the looking glass. So forcefully did she do so that she stumbled back a few feet—and in a most unladylike fashion plopped right down on her bottom.

"Curiouser and curiouser," she muttered.

As she pondered upon what had just occurred, she quite naturally began to wonder if her previous journey through this very same looking glass had not been a dream at all, but rather all too real.

Alice looked up at the rooftop rafters of the most beloved and only home she had ever known, and thought sadly about the fact that she was about to leave it forever.

"What have I got to lose?" she declared—then boldly stepped right through the shimmering looking glass.

The attic she left behind was empty now...save for the faint sounds of ghostly *laughter* in the same voice that had urged the sleeping Alice to come here in the first place.

Chapter 5

Alice experienced a slight dizzying sensation, as might be felt if one were spinning around while falling through the air at the same time.

She closed her eyes tightly until the sensation passed—just as her feet hit the ground and flipped out from under her, once again depositing her on her backside.

Being a proper young lady, Alice's first thought was that it was most *im*proper for a young lady to sit thus; so she quickly jumped to her feet.

She next and quickly noticed that she was no longer standing inside the attic of her family home. She wasn't inside at all; rather, she appeared to have landed in the middle of a lush and verdant forest.

This was most decidedly not Kensington Gardens. She suspected she was nowhere at all inside the limits of London: quite possibly nowhere in England. Nor was it nighttime, though dusk seemed rapidly approaching.

Brushing herself off, Alice began to explore her new environs. She did not do so recklessly, but it spoke highly of her character that neither was she timid. She accepted the seeming fact that she had somehow been transported to another world—with quite possibly no way back to her own—with the stoic resolve expected of a lady of good breeding.

At first glance, there did not appear to be anything untoward about her new environs. It could have been a forest found most anywhere in England (Or any number of other countries, for that matter). The air was cool, though not uncomfortably so, and cleaner smelling than that to which she was accustomed. (This was not surprising, given that Alice lived in an increasingly industrialized city teeming with people. Given the nature of the odors both industry and people are prone to produce, "clean" was a word that could seldom if ever be applied to the air hanging over London!)

Birds could be heard chirping and tweeting in the treetops, occasionally accompanied by the buzzing of various insects. In all, it did not appear to be an unpleasant place at all.

As the sun continued its inevitable decline and the forest began to darken, however, Alice admitted inwardly that she was becoming just the tiniest bit frightened.

As full darkness descended, Alice began to see tiny pinpoints of light not far from where she was. They were too low to be stars, and they seemed to flitter back and forth.

Some of the tiny lights fluttered near and round about her, and her ears picked up a faint sound as of the tinkling of tiny crystal bells.

When several of these mysterious lights seemed to coalesce together in a clump and start to slowly float toward her, Alice prudently backed away from them in consternation.

"Hello!" said an exuberant voice from directly behind her.

"Oh!" Alice exclaimed, spinning around.

"*Oh!*"

To Alice's amazement, she found herself face-to-face with a smiling *boy*—one who appeared to be hanging upside down in midair!

Smack!

Without conscious thought, Alice soundly *slapped* the boy. Taken by surprise, he fell headfirst to the forest floor.

At the sight of the boy unceremoniously sprawled on the ground, the gathering of lights fluttering round and about Alice began to give off a sound like that of tittering laughter coming from dozens of tiny throats.

Whatever that noise was, it proved to be infectious; for even the boy Alice had slapped began to laugh heartily, holding his belly and rolling back and forth.

This made Alice feel very bad for having struck him and she reached down, offering her hand to help him rise. He accepted it most graciously and bounded to his feet.

As the boy stood proudly in front of her, legs spread, hands on hips and a wide smile on his full lips, Alice took the time to look him over more closely.

He appeared to be close in age to her. In dress Alice would have described him as looking a bit like a blend of Robin Hood and descriptions she had read of North American Indian tribesmen.

The boy was shod in soft, deerskin moccasins. His torso was wrapped in an equally soft, sleeveless buckskin tunic that came halfway down his bare thighs and was cinched snugly around his waist by a wide, black leather belt.

Both tunic and moccasins were ornately decorated with intricate, colorful beadwork. A very long dagger rested in a silver scabbard that rode on the belt at his right hip.

From the lobe of one ear dangled a shiny earring. It was made from a gold coin: pieces of eight, Alice believed such coins were called.

What she did not know was that this piece of jewelry had originally been the property of an Italian *pirate* named Cecco. She would have been quite horrified to learn that the boy had come into possession of the earring by removing it from Cecco's *body*, after the pirate was slain in a fierce battle.

The boy's hair was somewhat long and unruly, in slight curls of ash blond (in contrast to Alice's brighter, more corn silk yellow hair that hung past her shoulders). Flower petals of different sorts peeked here and there out of the curls of the boy's hair, as did strands of thin, green vines.

His eyes were big, bright and blue, somewhat like Alice's own. Unlike hers, though, his danced with a definite air of mischief. Those eyes were nestled in the middle of a round face that could better be described as being pretty than as handsome; it was quite like the face of a young woman.

Hoping to make up for her previous lack of good manners, Alice curtsied to the boy.

"Please forgive me for having struck you," she said meekly. "It's just that you took me quite by surprise."

The boy in turn made an exaggerated bow at the waist. "It's quite all right," he said, in a voice that somehow sounded younger than he looked.

"No harm was done. After all—you *do* hit like a girl!"

"Well, I should hope *so*—since I *am* a girl!" Alice replied rather more hotly than she intended.

"Regardless," she continued stiffly, "striking you was not the proper thing to do. And one must try to be proper at all times."

"Why?" the boy retorted, snorting. "I'm almost *never* proper—and look how happy I am!"

"Be that as it may," Alice sniffed, "it was most unladylike of me; and I am glad I didn't hurt you." So saying, she reached out and laid the palm of her hand against the reddened cheek she had slapped.

At that, one of the tiny lights flittering about overhead separated itself from the rest of the flock and dived swiftly downward—bonking the unwary Alice right atop her head!

"Ouch!"

"Stop that!" the boy scolded, shaking a finger. The light that had struck Alice fluttered down to alight atop a nearby rock.

"What *is* that?" Alice demanded angrily, whilst rubbing the top of her head.

"'That' is *Tinker Bell*," the boy explained. "She's a friend of mine—but she *can* be a bit ugly some times."

"Ugly is right," Alice agreed, bending down to take a closer look at her attacker. Only then, and to her great surprise, did she realize that what she had thought to be some sort of lightning bug was no insect at all.

It was a *fairy*!

Standing no more than four inches tall, this particular fairy was decidedly female. She didn't look like a normal, human little girl, but rather like a fully-grown young woman: albeit very tiny in stature. From the middle of her back, between her shoulder blades, there sprouted a pair of *wings*: gossamer and lovely, like those of a dragonfly.

The fairy lady wore clothing that, by Alice's proper Victorian standards, was scandalously skimpy: nothing but tiny slippers and a skeleton leaf dress that was far too high on the bottom and far too low on the top, revealing far, far too much of what lay beneath.

Silken blond hair was pulled back and tied in a tail from a round face with large, almond shaped eyes and ripe lips. Her figure could rightly be called voluptuous and she had a slight bulging plumpness to her tummy.

The fairy still had a combative look about her, standing with clenched fists on her hips and glaring darkly up at Alice.

"Oh, my goodness," Alice whispered breathlessly. "Miss Tinker Bell... you're *beautiful*!"

At this admiring declaration, the little fairy's fists and face relaxed; she even seemed to smile slightly. With a soft, buzzing sound, her wings began to whir. She flitted up near the boy's ear and a tinkling sound emanated from her. The boy smiled in response.

"She says you don't have to call her 'Miss'," he told Alice. "You may call her Tinker Bell. Tink, if you like."

"I'd like that very much. But where are my manners? I haven't introduced *myself*. My name is Alice."

"And I," the boy said in a rather melodramatic tone of voice, "am *Peter Pan*."

"It's a pleasure to meet you, Peter," Alice said, and once again curtsied.

"Of course it is—I'm wonderful!"

"But not very modest," Alice huffed.

"Modesty is only for people who have nothing to be proud of."

Alice was sure she did not agree with that, but thought it would be impolite to say so. So instead she merely looked once more around her new surroundings.

"Is this Wonderland?" she asked.

"No," Pan replied. "This is *Neverland*."

"Hmm," Alice said, accepting that statement as easily as if the impish boy had said she was in London's East End; perhaps because a part of her thought this was all merely another dream.

"I wonder why my mirror brought me *here*?"

"A *mirror* brought you here?" Pan asked.

"In a manner of speaking. I stepped *through* the looking glass—and here I am."

"That sounds *most* unusual," Pan observed.

"Why? How did *you* get here?" Alice asked him.

"The same way I always do," he replied matter-of-factly, pointing up at the now fully dark night sky.

"I found the second star to the right—then flew straight on till morning!"

"Excuse me? You—*flew*?" Alice said incredulously.

In that moment it occurred to her that when she had first seen the boy he had been hanging upside down behind her. But she could now see that there was nothing directly overhead—no tree branch, no rope—that he could possibly have been hanging *from*!

"Naturally," Pan said with a shrug. "I fly most everywhere."

He then proceeded to demonstrate. Bending at the knees and then springing upward, he quickly and easily defied the law of gravity by rising effortlessly into the air, flittering in and out amidst the gathering of fairies before alighting back in front of Alice.

R.A. Jones

"That's wonderful!" Alice exclaimed, clapping her hands. "Tell me; how *far* can you fly?"

"It's not how far or how long you fly that matters," Pan replied. "It's how *high*!"

"Well then…how high can you fly?"

"To the stars!"

Alice thought on this for a moment. "Well, if you fly that *high*…haven't you also flown that *far*?"

"You're the most argumentative girl, aren't you?" Pan said, scowling.

"I don't think I am, no."

"Yet you'll argue about arguing," Pan declared.

Now it was Alice who scowled, though she decided to pursue this string of conversation no further.

"Can you tell me how it is that you are able to fly?" she asked.

"Strange as it may seem," Pan replied, "it is both incredibly easy and extremely difficult. In order to do it properly, you have to truly believe that you can fly—and be truly free.

"Since these are qualities only fully possessed by *children*—that means of course that only children can fly."

"So you won't be able to fly anymore once you've grown up?" Alice asked innocently.

Both Peter and the fairies laughed at that, filling the glen with a sparkling buzz that exuded joy.

"I have no intention of *ever* growing up!" Pan told Alice.

She frowned. "But how can you *not*? Everybody grows up!"

"Not if they don't want to," Pan declared. "And why would I ever want to?" The fairies swarming about again tittered.

"Most grown-ups," the boy explained condescendingly, "are just tall children who have forgotten how to have fun—and who want everybody else to forget, too!"

"But everyone has to grow up eventually," Alice insisted. "They have to face responsibility and all the other scary things in life."

"You don't think children have responsibilities?" Pan retorted. "And almost *everything* is scary to them." He then smiled a conspiratorial sort of smile.

"But it's worth it," he said, "to be *free*!"

Alice didn't understand. "Free to do *what*?"

"*To be alive!*" Pan shouted, spreading his arms to either side and spinning around twice.

Chapter 6

The little fairy Tinker Bell circled around Pan's head before lightly landing on his left shoulder near his ear. In the tinkling fairy language she swiftly communicated with him. He smiled and nodded.

"Tink just reminded me that we were about to have a *party* when you showed up," he told Alice.

"What sort of party?" she asked.

"A fun one!"

"But what is it that you are celebrating?"

"Who needs a *reason* to have a party?"

Alice opened her mouth to reply, then closed it and shrugged.

"So the only *real* question to ask," said Pan, "is would you like to join us?"

"I think I would!" Alice responded enthusiastically. It had been ever so long since she'd had any real fun, and she felt certain her poor parents would understand and approve if she left her grief behind if only for a little while.

Suddenly, seemingly from everywhere and nowhere, cheerful music filled the glen. The fairies began to "dance" by bobbing about in the air to the rhythm of the music.

The boy Peter had managed to avail himself of a five-reed *pan flute* and joined in with the merry melody. Even as he played, he danced a lively jig. Alice, laughing and clapping her hands in time with the music, could see that he was an excellent dancer.

"He really *is* wonderful, isn't he?" a small voice said close to Alice's ear. Alice was surprised when she turned her head and saw that the words had come from Tinker Bell.

"You can speak people speak!" Alice exclaimed.

"I can if I choose to," Tink replied. Even though the words she spoke were clear, they floated from her tongue more like musical notes.

"But since Peter understands and speaks fairy fluently and because there are very few people other than him I care to speak to—I usually don't."

"Then I am honored that you chose to speak to me," Alice said sincerely; and Tink found it very hard to hate this pretty girl, much as she would like to.

"Just a moment," Tink said, then flew away. When she returned she was carrying a "cup" in each hand. Though smaller in size than would be a thimble for a person's little finger, to a fairy each was a handful. Tink passed one to Alice.

Holding the cup delicately between thumb and forefinger so as not to crush it, Alice looked down at its contents. A lightly golden brown liquid swirled within.

"We call it *fairy nectar,*" Tink explained. "We make it from the honeysuckle that grows here in our forest. I think you'll like it."

"I'm sure I will," Alice replied, then raised her little cup. "A toast, then. To Miss Tinker Bell and all her fairy friends."

"And to Peter Pan!" Tink added enthusiastically.

Alice raised her cup to her lips and drank its entire contents in a single gulp. It did indeed taste like honey, but slightly different as well; it stung her throat a little as she swallowed it down.

"I'll get us another," Tink offered, taking Alice's empty cup from her and flying away.

Before she could return, though, Pan danced over to where Alice stood. Without missing a note on his flute, he reached out, took Alice by the hand and pulled her out to the center of the glen.

She stood there still and awkward at first before realizing that Peter and the fairies expected her to join them in their dance. She wasn't at all sure it would be proper to engage in such public cavorting but was almost sure it would be impolite *not* to.

Slowly at first, then with more confidence, she imitated the moves of the boy. She quickly found herself dancing with total abandon, pausing only now and again to accept another cup of nectar from Tink or one of the other fairies.

Alice couldn't have said how long she danced, but at length she found herself growing breathless and even a tiny bit light-headed. So she finally just threw herself on the grass, giggling. And happy, too; it had been so awfully long since she'd had any real fun.

Pan threw himself down on the sward beside her, dropping his flute and laughing with gusto. Tinker Bell, seeming to fly a bit erratically, landed on his shoulder; she too was laughing.

Alice, finding she needed to squint her eyes slightly to make them focus, noticed something odd about the other fairies. Their flight patterns seemed to have become as erratic as Tink's, to the point where they occasionally collided with each other in midair. Every time such a collision occurred, the tittering sound of fairy laughter grew louder.

"What's wrong with them?" Alice asked Peter.

"Nothing," Pan replied. "They're just a wee bit *tipsy,* that's all."

Tipsy. Alice recalled that was a term her parents had applied to great-aunt

Sophie when the elderly spinster helped herself to just a little too much of the cooking sherry.

"But how can they be?" Alice asked with puzzlement. "All they've been drinking is honey."

"*Fermented* honey," Pan replied. "To you and I, their tiny cups don't amount to much." He eyed Alice accusingly.

"Though I must say you've indulged in a *lot* of tiny cups!"

"But I didn't know it was alcoholic!" Alice cried defensively, blushing deeply.

"But to them," Pan continued, waving one hand carelessly in the direction of the carousing fairies, "it's like drinking goblets of ale!"

"Oh!" said Alice. "That's horrible! You shouldn't have allowed that to happen, Peter; it's not proper."

"Hmmph!" Tinker Bell, by now more than a wee bit tipsy herself, cast a jaundiced eye in Alice's direction. "Sounds to me like this girl came from *Dull*-land—or *Unhappy*-land."

"Worse," Pan replied, winking at Tink while tapping the side of his upturned nose with one finger.

"She came from the *Real* World!"

"*Eeeek!*" Tink responded with a mock shriek.

Stung by their words (she could never abide being teased, even when she, like them, was a wee bit tipsy), Alice angrily retorted, "Then I suppose that makes *this* the *Un*real World!"

"Oh, no, no, no, no, no!" Peter asserted. "Unreal World is another place entirely!"

Feeling flustered and frustrated, Alice declared, "How can it be a place at all, if it's unreal?"

"Because the unreal is just as real as the real is real—it just doesn't take itself so seriously!" the boy asserted smugly. He glanced down at Tinker Bell, who nodded firmly.

"Everybody knows that!" Tink avowed.

"And that's why the unreal world is better than the real world," Pan concluded. He then pretended to whisper to Tink, though deliberately doing so in a voice loud enough for Alice to hear.

"She's not very bright, is she?"

"I beg your pardon?" Alice said indignantly.

"There's no need to beg in Neverland," Peter crowed. "Anything you want will be freely given to you." He grinned wickedly.

"And if it isn't…why, then—you simply *steal* it!"

" ... YOU'VE INDULGED IN A LOT OF TINY CUPS!"

Pan and Tink both began to laugh as if this was the most uproarious statement ever uttered. Alice's only response was to sulk (something even proper girls were allowed to do when the occasion called for it).

She forgot her sulking moments later, when a small but bright new pinpoint of light suddenly erupted in the midst of the celebrating fairies. Its unannounced appearance caused the swarming fairies to burst out in a wave of little fairy cheers.

"What happened?" Alice asked. "What is it?"

"A new fairy has just been born!" Pan exclaimed.

"Huh? But—*how*?" Alice blurted out, then buried her face in her hands to conceal her embarrassment over her indelicateness in asking such a question. It was most unladylike.

"A newly born human baby somewhere has just laughed for the very first time," Pan said in wonderment.

"What?" This hadn't answered Alice's question at all.

"Every time a baby laughs for the first time," Pan explained, "a new fairy is born!"

"Oh, my," Alice gasped as the significance of that utterance set in. "There must be quite a few fairies, then."

"Not so many as you might think," Pan said wistfully. "You see, every time a human child stops believing in things like fairies—a fairy *dies*."

"Oh, no!" Alice cried. "That's terrible!"

"Especially if you're a fairy," Pan said philosophically.

"Of course," he continued, "fairies tend not to live very long in any event—because of their small size, I imagine."

"Oh, dear!" Alice said, then leaned in closer to Peter.

"What about poor Tink?" she asked in a true whisper. "How long has she lived already?"

"Oh, Tink's quite *old*, actually," Peter replied—*not* in a whisper.

"Hmmmph!" Tinker Bell hmmmphed.

"By fairy standards, I mean," Pan had sense enough to quickly amend. "She's lived far longer than most fairies do; I don't know why."

The boy then found himself distracted by the strains of a fresh new song floating from the flock of fairies: a song meant to welcome the newest arrival into fairydom. Pan rushed off to join in the good cheer.

Alice took note of the way Tinker Bell gazed longingly after Peter as he left. The girl felt her own heart aching as she leaned closer to the little fairy.

"Does Peter *really* not know why you linger on here with him, Tink?" she asked softly.

Tink shrugged and tried to smile. "He's a silly ass," she stated firmly, even as her diaphanous wings began to flutter and lift her up into the air.

"But he's mine."

The forlorn fairy had barely started toward the rest of her flock when Alice heard a loud hissing sound intruding upon the merriment; it was almost like the warning sounds of a dozen venomous snakes.

Alice's eyes were drawn to a movement and she lowered her gaze to see three black, metal orbs come rolling into the middle of the glen.

Each was about the size of a grapefruit, and each had a burning *fuse* attached to it.

"*Cannon balls!*" Pan shouted at the top of his lungs.

Chapter 7

Pan launched himself through the air, wrapping his arms around Alice and dragging her with him to the ground. Holding her tightly, he began to roll away from the center of the glen.

Before he could completely do so, all three of the cannon balls (for that is indeed what they were) exploded—sending out billows of dark smoke and waves of piercing, nerve wracking sound.

So awful was the noise that it instantly rendered all the fairies inert and they dropped to the ground.

Peter and Alice writhed in pain on the sward, clutching at their ears, clenching their eyes shut as they nearly blacked out themselves.

When the pounding in Pan's brain subsided to no more than a harsh ringing in his ears, he at last opened his eyes again. When he did—he found a large, dangerous-looking *cutlass* pointed right at his face.

"*Smee!*" he exclaimed in disbelief.

Pan recognized the short, portly Irishman who had served as bo'sun under the infamous pirate called *Captain Hook*. Pan and his companions, known as the *Lost Boys*, had engaged the crew of Hook's ship the *Jolly Roger* in a fierce and bloody battle. When it ended, Hook and all his crew—save for Smee and one other—had met their deaths.

How long ago this had happened Pan couldn't say; time had almost no meaning for the perpetual boy. But he remembered Smee well.

"Sure and you'd best be lyin' still, lad," Smee now warned in a raspy voice, "else you'll be feelin' the point o' *Johnny Corkscrew* in yer gizzard!" ("Johnny

Corkscrew" being the name by which Smee called his cutlass. Why he felt the need to give a name to a sword, no one but Smee could tell you.)

Smee held the cutlass in his right hand; clutched in his left was a sputtering torch. As Pan looked about, he saw three more torch-bearing pirates enter the glen; each one looked a bit like Smee and each one also carried a wicked cutlass.

Smoke from the exploded cannonballs still lingered, swirling about and creating eerie shadows from the torchlight. From behind this smoky curtain, a royal figure now emerged.

Pan thought it was a *woman* but he wasn't sure at first, for a hundred beams of light seeming to stream from her made it almost painful to gaze upon her.

A thin crown at her brow circled highly piled hair that was as black as a raven's wing, and the crown was laden with diamonds. The same was true of the elegant black gown she wore. It trailed all the way to the ground, hugging every curve of her enticing form, and the swirling patterns of diamonds sewn into its velvet cloth reflected and magnified the light from the torches now illuminating the glen.

The woman (for such she obviously was) was stunningly beautiful of face, but it was the kind of beauty that evil often hides within and behind. Like a statue that has physical perfection but no life. Her eyelids were painted a light blue above dark eyes; her lips were deep red and cruel.

Almost as striking as her appearance was the fact that, waddling along beside her like a reptilian pet was a *crocodile*. The beast was enormous: at least fifteen feet long. Maybe twenty. Yet, in the woman's presence, it seemed docile as a poodle.

This regal lady walked (glided?) to where Pan still lay on the ground. Bending over, she carefully studied his defiant face. She did not appear to be impressed by what she saw.

"I am *Sangramore*," she said in a haughty voice that, like all of her, lacked the warmth of an icy river.

"I am the *Queen of Diamonds*."

She then happened to cast her eyes upon Alice. "And you I already know," she said to the girl's surprise.

"You're a bit older now, Alice—but no less *stiff*."

"I'm quite sure I would remember if we'd ever met, Your Majesty," Alice said respectfully. After all, being a seeming captive did not free you from observing all the proprieties.

"I didn't say we'd ever *met*, you silly little girl. I said that I know you." The queen smiled, but it was a smile that did not travel from her lips to her eyes.

"You were in Wonderland, weren't you?"

Alice was amazed by this declaration. "That's not possible," she gasped. "Wonderland only existed in my dreams!"

"Oh, darling," Sangramore said, stroking Alice's hair in a manner that brought chills rather than comfort. "All of life is but a dream (exactly what the poet had said). That doesn't make it any less real, now does it?"

Here we go again, thought Alice, without voicing that thought.

"But you managed to escape from that horrid place," the queen went on. "Just as I finally did."

"Why would you want to escape?" Alice asked.

Sangramore leaned in uncomfortably close to the girl. "Because the place is *mad*. Didn't you notice when you were there, my dear? All of it. And every creature that lived there was *just* as mad.

"Except *me*, of course."

Her words brought back a nearly forgotten memory to Alice. On one of her imaginary (but now, she knew, not so imaginary) journeys to Wonderland she had encountered an oddly compelling beast called the *Cheshire Cat*.

"We're all mad here," the cat had told her. (Yes, in Wonderland, cats and other animals could speak as well as you or I. Or I, at least.) "I'm mad. You're mad."

Alice was beginning to think the cat had been right.

"At last, though," Sangramore said, interrupting Alice's thoughts, "I found a way to escape the insanity—and traveled to *this* lovely place."

"But—if I may ask—what possible reason could you have for attacking us?" Alice inquired, still maintaining a polite tone of voice.

"Dear Alice. I'm a *queen*, darling. That means I don't have to have any reason at all—for doing anything I please!

"It just so happens, though," she said, straightening up to her full and not inconsiderable height, "that I have a very, very good reason. Before I tell you, I would like you to meet my second-in-command."

Sangramore dramatically waved one arm. As if silently summoned, a previously unseen person stepped forward through the concealing veil of smoke.

"No…" Pan choked.

Posturing most grandly no more than ten feet away from Pan stood the boy's greatest enemy.

Captain James Hook!

Atop the pirate's head sat a bright, blue tri-corner hat from which dangled an ostrich feather; black ringlets of hair escaped from the bottom of the hat and ran down to his shoulders. A large, satin overcoat with large ivory buttons fell to the top of his calves; his entire style of dress seemed meant to evoke images and memories of the former British monarch Charles II. Hook's left hand clutched a tall walking stick that was topped by a small, silver carving of an eagle's head.

Hook had been described more than once as having a handsome countenance, but in truth he had the cold appeal that death itself holds for some people (not you or I, of course). His face, with its prominent Roman nose and high cheekbones amidst otherwise cadaverous features, was framed around blue eyes that spoke of perpetual melancholy.

From his harsh lips hung an odd contraption: a holder with twin apertures from which protruded two dark, thin cigars that he was puffing upon simultaneously.

"No!" Peter gasped. "You can't be here!"

"And yet, obviously—I *am*!" Hook declared gleefully. Shifting his gaze to Alice, he lightly tapped the side of his head. Alice shuddered to see that the "hand" the pirate used to do this was not a hand at all—but rather a large, deadly *hook* that rested at the end of his arm where his right hand should have resided.

"He *does* have the mind of a child, y'know," he said in reference to Peter.

"It gives him a deliciously wicked sense of humor—but sometimes prevents him from grasping that which is right before his eyes."

"But," Pan stuttered, "but I killed you myself!"

"Did you really?"

"*Most* really!"

"To be completely fair—which I seldom am," Hook told him, "*I* thought you had too, dear boy." He stepped in closer.

"*Here's* a thought," the pirate ruminated. "Perhaps I *can't* die—at least so long as you and all your cockiness still live." With almost delicate steps, he moved still closer to where Pan sat on the forest floor.

"But," Hook continued, "in addition to being rakishly handsome and a master at playing the harpsichord—" He turned toward Alice. "My playing can make a tax collector weep," then back to Pan.

"I am also an excellent *swimmer*—especially for a man with only one hand!" he shouted.

"You took *that* away from me, remember, Pan?" the pirated said coldly, glaring at the equally cold iron hook that had taken the place of his real hand.

Pan had severed it and part of Hook's arm with a stroke of his long dagger during one of their earlier battles. Adding insult to injury, the boy had then fed the severed limb to the very beast that now stood beside the Queen of Diamonds.

At the climax of what both thought would be their final confrontation, Pan had stabbed Hook and sent him plunging off the deck of his ship the *Jolly Roger*. The crocodile—who had taken to stalking Hook in hopes of finishing him off—had been waiting in the water below. Pan had of course presumed the worst.

Rather than meekly accepting that he was doomed to become the main course on the crocodile's dinner menu, though, Hook had fiercely staved off the beast and frantically paddled toward shore.

As good fortune sometimes favors even those who don't deserve it, the pirate had discovered a small cave that offered him refuge. The rocky ground along the shore leading up to it was steep and slippery; but his namesake hook allowed him to climb up and out of the water.

"So in a way," Hook said, momentarily interrupting his narrative, smiling and slowly waving his iron appendage back and forth in front of Peter's face, "I have you to thank for saving my life, boy!"

The crocodile, for all its prodigious strength, had been unable to find enough purchase to climb up after the pirate captain. But it had patiently remained nearby, effectively making the cave Hook's prison. Hook managed to survive by eating crabs that crawled up into the cave at high tide and by drinking the water that oozed from the walls of the cave. In time, even the wound Peter had inflicted on him healed. (Even it proved useful in a way, for its aching in his shoulder allowed Hook to predict when rain was about to fall!)

Yet it was a most miserable form of existence Hook endured, made only slightly more bearable by engaging in the mental exercise of imagining all the many different ways he might torture the hated Peter Pan if ever the opportunity arose.

And at long last, Hook's maddening, solitary confinement had ended, when the Queen of Diamonds had rescued him and made him her partner.

"And now we have you, you wretch," Hook said, making a sweeping gesture with the walking stick in his left hand. As he did so, the crocodile at Sangramore's side lunged forward, snapping at the pirate's arm.

"Keep that walking suitcase away from me!" Hook shrieked.

In response, Sangramore went down on one knee and began to lightly scratch the crocodile under its long chin. The reptile's eyes closed and it made a contented noise that sounded like a cat with rocks in its throat purring.

"You really can't blame him," the queen said, excusing her pet's behavior. "It's not *his* fault he's developed a taste for *pirate*." Hook gulped loudly.

"*That's* your fault, too!" he screeched at Pan. "It wasn't enough that you cut off the better part of my arm; oh, no. Then you had to go and feed it to *him*!"

Peter shrugged. "Well, Hook…crocs have to eat, *too*."

Hook roared in rage and reared back to strike Pan with his hook.

"Ah-ah-ah-ah," Sangramore admonished, and Hook grudgingly lowered his arm. Sangramore patted her pet crocodile atop his scaly head.

"Who's a good boy?" she crooned, then looked straight at Pan. "Oh, but my poor baby here had the hardest time eating *anything* for the longest time. All because he had the misfortune of swallowing that blasted *clock*!"

Peter remembered the wind-up clock well. Even while in the belly of the beast, its ticking could be clearly heard. It was the tick-tick-tick of the clock that alerted Captain Hook whenever the crocodile was close by; after awhile there were times when the pirate heard it in his head even when the creature was nowhere around.

"Even after the clock had run down and stopped ticking," Sangramore explained, "it still just sat there in the poor dear's tummy.

"It was stuck there, you see, so he couldn't pass it. It took up so much room that his stomach would barely accept enough food for him to survive and it made everything he did eat taste simply awful; rather like iron filings filtered through dirty socks, I would imagine."

The queen continued prattling on, though by this time Pan was barely listening to her; his thoughts were already turning to how he might escape. Sangramore explained that—using the sort of wiles that are so useful to monarchs and salesmen—she had succeeded in extracting the hated clock from the crocodile's belly.

As a result, the reptilian carnivore was utterly devoted to her, to the point of (mostly) suppressing its frequent urges to take a bite out of Captain Hook.

"I didn't have much to come back to once I got out of that infernal cave," Hook said, wishing to draw attention away from the vile crocodile.

"Thanks to you and those blasted Lost Boys of yours, most of my crew had gone to Davy Jones' Locker. Fortunately, Mr. Smee survived—and it turned out he had three brothers who were of an equally piratical bent." Smee puffed his chest out proudly.

"It's not *much* of a crew, y'know," Hook went on in a stage whisper, causing

Smee's chest to deflate. "But in hard times, one takes what one can get."

"And I suppose now you intend to kill *me*," Pan said, causing Alice to gasp. Having fully recovered from the effects of the cannon ball blast, the boy was now back on his feet, looking cocky as ever.

"May I?" Hook asked almost pleadingly, looking back over his shoulder at the haughty Queen of Diamonds.

"Not yet, pet," Sangramore said in a soothing voice, reaching out and lightly stroking Hook's chin. (The queen already had the pirate as enthralled as she did her other pet, the crocodile, Alice observed.)

"We need him, remember?"

So saying, the queen turned her back on all of them and dipped one hand down into the bodice of her sparkling gown.

When she turned back around, she was holding in that hand a rolled, parchment scroll that she held out to Pan.

"Upon this scroll," she explained, "there is written a *riddle*: the first in a series of *six* such riddles. Each riddle leads to the next riddle—with the final riddle leading the way to a great *treasure!*"

"What *sort* of treasure?" Alice asked sensibly.

"That, I don't really know," the queen admitted. "But it must be very valuable—else it wouldn't really be a treasure, now would it?"

"No, I suppose not."

"But it is rumored to be most fabulous," Sangramore continued, "and so I must have it!" She stared intently at Pan before pointing one long finger with a similarly long, darkly red nail directly at him.

"And I want *you* to find it for me."

"Me? Why me?" Peter asked.

"Because James (the pirate captain so loved it when her majesty deigned to call him by his first name) told me, somewhat begrudgingly, that you are a very clever boy. And solving any good riddle requires cleverness."

"Aren't *you* clever?" Alice asked her.

"Oh, aren't you sweet? No, little girl. You see, it's actually quite *dangerous* for a royal to be clever; it makes others want to kill them. It's far smarter to simply be regal.

"And I think you will admit—I *am* a regal royal."

"You are, Your Majesty." (Alice just couldn't help being proper, even to such an evil royal.)

"And why should I help you find this treasure?" Pan now asked defiantly.

"Why? Yes, why?" The queen pondered for a moment. "Oh, yes; I almost forgot." She snapped her fingers at one of the nearby pirates, who leaped forward holding what appeared to be a small, empty *birdcage*; no larger than might be needed to hold a sparrow.

Taking the cage from him, Queen Sangramore knelt down beside where the fallen and still largely senseless Tinker Bell lay. With surprising tenderness she cupped the stricken fairy in her hand—and placed her inside the cage, locking the gate closed.

"You have one week, Pan," Sangramore then said in a voice that could crack stone. "One week to find and solve all the riddles.

"Seven days to find the treasure, bring it to me and place it in my hands—or I feed your little girlfriend to my pet!"

As if it understood completely what its mistress had just said, the crocodile licked its scaly lips and growled expectantly.

Alice, being fairly clever herself, stepped forward boldly.

"How do you know for sure there really *is* such a treasure—and that those other riddles even exist?"

"Mr. Smee?" Sangramore prompted, looking at the bo'sun; he was still holding his cutlass on Pan.

"During my travels," the little Irishman recounted, "after the disappearance of my cap'n, I happened to come upon an aged, dyin' pirate. That alone was enough of a bona fide for me; any pirate strong enough and tough enough to live long enough to die of old age ain't gonna bother lyin' to a fellow pirate."

(Alice failed to see the logic in that statement, but chose to keep such doubts to herself.)

"He had nothin' ta gain by lyin' ta me," Smee continued (an opinion Alice found easier to believe), "and no reason ta have a false scroll on hand or to make up a story about treasure. There had been rumors of just such a treasure floatin' about for some time."

"That part at least is true," Pan whispered to Alice. "I've heard them myself!"

"Mr. Smee in turn gave the riddle to me," Captain Hook said, picking up the narrative. He then glared at the Irishman.

"Which still isn't enough to make me forget that he's been going about spreading the fable that he was the only man alive who *I* was afraid of!"

"A man's got ta eat, Cap'n," Smee said pleadingly. "Tellin' tall tales at yer expense for the amusement of the locals in exchange for a few pennies was all I had!"

"You'd better *hope* the treasure is real," Queen Sangramore snarled, interrupting the pirates' quarrel. "Because real or not…the snotty little fairy—"

"*Hey*!" objected a groggy but thoroughly insulted Tinker Bell.

"In one week—the little fairy *dies*!"

Chapter 8

"ook and I will have your fairy friend aboard the *Jolly Roger*," Sangramore concluded, "sailing a random course while you search for the treasure. On the seventh day, we will weigh anchor in Pirate's Cove.

"Meet us there with the treasure—or else."

The villains then took their leave, fading back into the trees until there was no trace of them save for a chilling cackle coming from the wicked Queen of Diamonds.

"Why do they always have to laugh?" Pan muttered.

"What are you going to do, Peter?" Alice asked.

"What can I do?" the boy replied. "Tink is my bestest most best friend; I have to save her."

"Why, then, we'd best start by solving the riddle the queen gave you," Alice said firmly. "What does the scroll say?"

Rather hesitantly, she thought, Pan unrolled the scroll. He stared at it most studiously for quite some time but said nothing.

"Well?" Alice finally prompted impatiently. "What does it say?"

To her surprise, Pan's shoulders slumped in seeming defeat and his arms fell uselessly to his sides.

"I don't know," he admitted in shame. "I can't read it."

"Why not?" Alice asked, unable to fully comprehend what he was saying. "Is it in some foreign tongue?"

"I don't know!" Pan snapped at her. "I don't know…because I can't *read*, all right? I can't read and I can't write!"

"Oh, no," Alice said softly and sympathetically. "How is such a thing possible?"

"It's *very* possible—if no one ever taught you *how*!"

"Oh. Oh. I'm sorry, Peter. Truly I am. But it's not your fault." She reached out and took the scroll from Pan's unresisting fingers.

"Here; maybe I can read it for you." She studied what was written upon the scroll for a minute, glad to find it was in English, then began to read the words aloud.

In the place where land is lost and found,
Look to the west and see three round.
Left and right will do no good; the middle one is best.
But linger not within too long, lest it will end your quest.

"I read the words completely right," Alice said. "But I'm afraid the riddle means nothing to me."

"It does to me, though," Pan said firmly. He took the scroll back from the girl.

"I have to go now, Alice. You can stay here with the fairies."

"What? No—absolutely not. I'm going with you!"

"It could be dangerous," he warned. "Especially for a girl."

"No more so than for a boy!" she argued.

"But why do you want to come along? Why should you care what happens to Tink?"

"Because I like her! I know we've only just met, but I like her; we girls have to stick together.

"Besides…no one should ever be fed to a crocodile. It's just not done in proper society; except possibly in Parliament." She was just getting warmed up.

"And don't forget," she reminded Pan, "the queen told us there would be *more* riddles to come. Who will read them if I don't come with you?" She noticed Peter flinch and wished she had worded that last line a bit more diplomatically.

"Why, even when you find the treasure you might need help carrying it. Given that the lady wears a king's ransom in diamonds—I would think it might take a very large treasure to so entice her that she would kidnap a fairy in order to obtain it!"

At this point, Alice had to pause to take a breath and Pan used the opportunity to speak himself.

"I can't deny the truth in everything you said," he conceded. "So I have made a decision.

"I think it would be best if you came with me, Alice."

"A very wise decision, Peter," Alice said graciously and saw him smile at the compliment.

"Let's go, then!" he cried and leaped up into the air.

"Wait!" Alice called after him. Pan stopped, "standing" in midair and looking down at her quizzically.

"What is it?" he asked.

"Have you forgotten?" Alice said. "I can't fly!"

Sighing impatiently, Pan flew back to ground. He put one arm around Alice's waist while she flung both arms around his neck.

"Hold on tight," he instructed her.

"Oooh!" she gasped as he leaped into the sky, carrying her with him.

Nothing else she had experienced in life could have prepared her for the sensation of flying through the air beyond the bounds of the earth. The wind rushing past her face felt cleaner and fresher than any air she'd ever breathed. Her body lost any sense of its own weight. If flying felt this liberating, this joyous to the birds of the air, Alice wondered why they ever bothered to land at all! Why not just fly forever?

Her first flight did not last nearly long enough to suit Alice. Within just a few minutes, Pan descended toward a small stand of tall trees. Near the top of one of the trees, Alice saw a small hut nestled. Pan alit on its spacious front landing and led Alice inside.

It was a Spartan habitation with only three small rooms and a ceiling barely high enough to walk under; but it was clean and neatly kept.

"Whose house is this?" Alice asked.

"Mine and Tink's."

"Together?" Alice asked, her Victorian sensibilities shocked. "I mean—together?"

"When we're both here, yes," Pan said casually. "We need to gather some supplies; we don't know but that we'll be gone the whole week."

He loaded a rucksack with breadfruits, yams and bananas and handed the sack to Alice. From a rain barrel on the front landing he filled two calabashes with water. He hung one around Alice's neck and the other around his own.

Finally, from a small footlocker on the floor near his bed, Pan pulled out a well-kept flintlock *pistol*, along with a powder horn and small pouch of shot.

"I don't use this very often," he told Alice as he slid the pistol into his broad belt. "Mostly because I don't know how to make gunpowder and balls for it." He glanced around the hut, assuring himself he had forgotten nothing essential.

"I've been stealing both as I needed them from the powder magazine aboard the *Jolly Roger*," he further explained. "It had been just floating there anchored and empty since the battle where I thought I killed Captain Hook.

"The last time I flew over Pirate's Cove, though, I noticed the ship was not there. I gave it little thought at the time; I just figured it had somehow slipped its anchor and drifted off with the tide. Now I know better."

Pan led the way back onto the landing. As Alice dared to look down from the heights, she noticed something a bit peculiar.

"Some of the other trees 'round here," she observed, pointing down. "They have *holes* near their bases, like the mouths of caves. What are they?"

"They're the openings that lead down to an underground dwelling place… where the *Lost Boys* used to live," Pan said. Alice detected a certain sadness mixed with bitterness in Peter's voice.

"Who are the Lost Boys?" she asked tentatively.

"They're nobody now," he said rather contemptuously. "They were just what the name says: boys from out in the Real World who became lost and had nowhere to go. So I took them in.

"There have been quite a few of them. Some died or were killed here; some were stupid enough to let themselves grow up and leave." It was clear Pan held little truck with the latter.

"It didn't matter, for there were always new boys to take their place. Until the last batch." His voice faded slightly.

"They abandoned me to go back and be adopted by the Darling family." Alice didn't know if "darling" was the name of the family or merely a flattering description of them, but she thought it wisest not to inquire.

"They decided they would rather have parents and go to school and grow up than to stay here and have adventures!" Pan's voice now had a mocking edge.

"For some reason—I don't know why—no more Lost Boys have yet come to take their place."

"Is it really *so* bad to grow up, Peter?" Alice asked softly, placing a hand on his arm. He pulled away from her.

"It is if it means you can never fly again!"

Alice now desperately wanted to change the subject. "I forgot to ask you, Peter. The riddle Queen Sangramore gave us; do you know what it means?"

"She said I was clever," Pan said absently, then shook himself and smiled wanly. "I understood it the moment you read it. It was directions intended to send us to a very specific place."

"And what place would that be?"

"Where else? *The Mermaids' Lagoon!*"

Chapter 9

There really *are* mermaids!" Alice exclaimed.

"Of course there are," Pan replied. "Why else do you suppose they would call this Mermaids' Lagoon?"

"Well," Alice deflected, "they sometimes call Gibraltar the Pillars of Hercules—but Hercules isn't really there."

"Have you ever been to Gibraltar?"

"No, but—"

"Then how can you be *sure* Hercules isn't there?"

There was no suitable reply Alice could think of for that, so unlike most people in such situations, she said nothing.

She and Pan were still flying a good hundred feet in the air, but now over placid blue waters rather than land. Directly below them, a large flat rock rose about twelve inches out of the water.

And lying languidly atop the rock, seemingly sunning themselves, were four young women who could indeed only be described as mermaids!

"Hello!" Peter called down to them as he began his descent.

With a shrill cry, three of the mermaids hurled themselves off the rock and into the water. The last part of them to disappear beneath the rolling waves was their large, fishy *tails*.

"Don't take their reaction personally," Peter assured Alice. "They have good reason to fear people. I suspect I'm the only creature with legs they like!"

The fourth mermaid, though looking like she too could bolt at any moment, remained lying on the rock as Alice and Peter came to a soft and graceful landing.

Alice didn't know about other mermaids, but she felt sure by the look in this one's eyes that this particular mermaid did indeed like at least *one* creature with legs. She smiled brightly as Pan approached her.

That smile revealed white teeth that seemed unusually *pointed* to Alice. Perhaps in testimony to what mermaids had to *eat*, she thought.

"Millisandra," Pan said, stepping closer to the mermaid, "it's good to see you."

"It's always good to see you, Peter," Millisandra said with ardent sincerity.

"This is my new friend, Alice," Pan said, motioning for the girl to draw closer.

"What are you *staring* at, human?" the mermaid said harshly, noticing that Alice's gaze was not upon her upper body.

"Oh—please forgive me," Alice stammered. "It's just that...well, I've never seen a real, live mermaid before."

"Does that mean you *have* seen a *dead* one?" Millisandra bristled.

"No! Oh, goodness no! I've never seen *any* mermaid before!"

"Well, now you have. What do you think?"

"I'm amazed."

"As well you should be."

"Could I," Alice stammered, hesitantly stepping closer. "That is, may I… would you mind if I touched your *tail*?"

"I most certainly *would* mind!" Millisandra snapped. "How would you feel if I asked to touch *your* tail?"

Pan laughed at the very idea, while Alice flung her hands up to cheeks burning with embarrassment.

"I'm so *sorry*," she cried. "You're absolutely right, ma'am…that was a *horrid* thing for me to suggest!"

Millisandra's features softened slightly, though she was enjoying Alice's discomfort.

"I forgive you, girl," she said with feigned magnanimity. "Because you're Peter's friend—and because you don't know any better." She dramatically lifted the lower, fin-shaped end of her tail, then slapped it wetly upon the rock.

"You may touch my tail if you like."

"May I really?"

"I've said so."

As Alice slowly stepped closer, she more keenly examined the totality of the mermaid. From the waist up, she looked like an attractive young woman who had just emerged from a dip in the ocean.

Her skin was a light olive color and seemed almost to shine as sunlight danced off the many beads of water coating her. Her hair had a greenish tint and hung loosely down to and below her shoulders. Her only apparent article of clothing was a sort of halter-top set off by two gleaming seashells.

From the waist down, her body was indeed like that of a fish, scales and all. As she drew nearer still, Alice began to *smell* the mermaid. There was nothing remotely fishy or offensive about the odor; in fact, Millisandra smelled rather like freshly laundered sheets that have just been hung out to dry.

Kneeling down, Alice ran her hand slowly and softly along the mermaid's tail. She had felt fish scales before; the cook back home would sometimes allow the child to help in the kitchen.

These felt nothing at all like that, though. Even though she could clearly see the overlapping layers of what appeared to be scales, they felt more like moist silk to the touch.

"Marvelous," she uttered in awe.

"I like to think so," Millisandra said flippantly.

" . . . WOULD YOU MIND IF I TOUCHED YOUR TAIL ? "

"May I ask," Alice said, rising back to her feet. "Are there also mer*men* living here?"

Millisandra gasped, looking astounded. "Mer*men*?" she barked. "Who ever heard of such a thing? Why on earth or sea would we need mer*men*?"

"Forgive her," Peter said to his finny friend. "She isn't very bright."

"I am *so*!" Alice pouted, stomping one foot on the rock. "I'll have you know, I've enjoyed a very well-rounded, proper British education!"

"Ahh," said the mermaid. "That explains it. I forgive you."

Too angry to make any reply to this, Alice simply folded her arms across her breast and plopped down atop the rock.

"So, why have you come to visit, Peter?" Millisandra asked, ignoring Alice. "Are you here to play some games?"

"I wish I was," Peter said sadly. He then told Millisandra about all that had transpired and of his need to find the treasure demanded by Queen Sangramore.

"I'm afraid I don't know anything about any treasure being around here," Millisandra told him. "But you're free to look for it as long as you'd like."

"I never asked," Alice said, standing back up. "What led you to come here in the first place?"

"Because of the spot where we're standing," Peter explained. "This is called *Marooner's Rock*. At high tide, it sinks beneath the water, then rises back up again when the tide goes out."

"When land is lost and found," Alice whispered, quoting from the riddle.

"Exactly. That's how it got its name. Mutinous pirates would be marooned here—and drown when the tide came in.

"Now we have to look to the west," he said, walking to the middle of the rock and turning around. Sure enough, even though they were quite some distance from shore, in the face of the cliffs lining it he could see the entrances to three *caves*.

"The riddle said to ignore the ones on either side—so we need to go into the cave in the middle."

"I wouldn't do that if I were you, Peter," Millisandra warned.

"Why not? What's in there?"

"No one knows. Strange sounds issue from inside it, so we've always stayed away from it."

"Well, I'm going in," Pan declared stoutly. "How 'bout you?" he asked Alice.

"If you're willing, so am I."

"I really wish you wouldn't," said Millisandra.

"It'll be all right," Pan assured her. "And next time I come here—it *will* be to play games!"

He then looped his arm around Alice and sprang into the air. As they flew away from Marooner's Rock, Millisandra began to sing an eerie song. Alice couldn't understand any of the words of the song, but in tone it sounded like a funeral dirge. She shivered slightly.

"Wait here," Pan told Alice, setting her down when he reached the rocks just outside the cave. "I'll only be a minute."

Alice wasn't at all happy about being left alone, but it was indeed only a brief time. When Pan returned, he was carrying with him a short, dead tree branch and some dry moss.

He tightly wrapped the moss around one end of the branch. Kneeling down, he opened his powder horn and sprinkled a few precious grains of the gunpowder into the moss.

In a small leather pouch that rode on his belt, Pan always kept a *strike-a-light*: flint and steel used in the making of fire. It only took two strikes to ignite the powder and set the moss ablaze. They now had a serviceable torch.

"Are you ready?" Pan asked Alice.

"Whither thou goest," she said softly.

Taking that to be a "yes," and holding his torch above and ahead of him, Pan boldly led the way into the menacing cavern.

Chapter 10

Pan's makeshift torch cast enough light for them to see where to place their feet, but not much more. Shadows, because they conceal things, are often rather frightening; and there were plenty of shadows in this cave. The path was slippery, for water droplets constantly fell from the cavernous ceiling.

Then there was the noise. Sounding like the hissing of steam pipes, it came from somewhere ahead of them, from out of the darkness. Alice instinctively reached out and took hold of Peter's arm.

"See?" he said with a slight grin. "Children have *plenty* to be scared of."

"Yes," Alice concurred. "But if we were grown-ups instead—we might have sense enough to run away from here!"

Pan laughed heartily, but by the time the echoes of that laughter returned to them it had lost its mirth.

They continued onward for what, to Alice, seemed an agonizingly long time. Finally, deep inside the mysterious cave they came upon a series of stone steps. They did not appear to be natural but rather purposely hewn by some builder's hand ages ago.

At the top of the steps stood a small, stone column, no more than three feet tall. What appeared to be almost a nest of dark vines was wrapped round and round the base of the column. Atop the column sat a small wooden chest about the size of a lady's jewelry box.

"I'll wager that chest holds the next clue to finding the treasure," Alice surmised.

"I imagine you're right," Pan said. "Go and get it."

"What?" Alice said.

"Go and get it," the boy repeated. "I'll keep a lookout for any danger."

"Oh. Well…I suppose that does make sense." Alice didn't sound so sure.

Nonetheless, she released her grip on Peter's arm and began to tentatively climb the stone steps. Pan followed her up the first two steps, then stopped and turned his back to her in case something might come up behind them. He held his torch high in his left hand, while his right gripped the hilt of his dagger.

As Alice took one step at a time upward, the hissing sounds grew louder all around her.

"I'm not afraid," she whispered aloud to bolster her courage. "I'm not afraid, I'm not afraid, I'm not afraid."

But of course she was very much afraid.

But she was also very brave, too (after all, there is no point in courage save as a response to fear), and so she kept moving steadily up the stone staircase until she at last reached the pedestal upon which sat the chest.

Alice slowly reached toward it until her fingers touched its surface. It felt a bit slimy, more so than if it had simply been wet from all the dripping water. Her hands closed around it and lifted it from its perch. Turning around, she raised the chest over her head.

"I have it!" she cried triumphantly, her voice ringing off the cavernous walls around her.

That's when the large "nest" entwined around the stone pedestal began to move.

As they uncoiled of their own volition, Alice could now see that she was actually standing in the midst of a pit of *vipers*!

She had once seen an enormous snake on display at the London Zoo and recalled it was called an anaconda. Compared to the half dozen serpents that now rose up all around her, that beast now seemed no more formidable than the average garden snake.

Alice let out a heartfelt scream as one of the giant serpents whipped its coils around her waist and lifted her up in the air. The snake raised its intended victim toward its massive head. As if on hinges, its jaws opened widely, revealing long and jagged fangs crowded atop each other in its maw.

Maintaining her grip on the chest she had snatched from the pedestal, Alice now swung it with all the might she could muster. The giant serpent screeched as the chest connected with the side of its head, but it did not release its hold on the girl.

Other serpents rose up on all sides of her, vying for the best position to strike at her. Some of them even snapped at each other to stave off competition.

"Help me, Peter!" Alice cried.

Pan was already on his way to do just that, flying agilely up while dodging the thrashing tails and heads of the ravenous serpents. As he came, he lashed out right and left with both his torch and the drawn dagger he now held in his right hand.

Alice's heart skipped several beats as she found herself staring straight into the merciless eyes of the serpent that held her captive in its coils. It had fully recovered from the blow Alice had delivered and was more determined than ever to sink its fangs into her.

Its head darted forward—and at that very instant Pan rose up from beneath it, driving the tip of his dagger into the underside of the beast's head.

The giant snake thrashed about in pain and its coils loosened from around Alice, allowing her to drop to the floor of the cavern.

"Run, Alice!" Peter yelled down at her. "Get out of here!"

For once, Alice had not the slightest inclination to argue with him. Clutching the chest tightly and dodging whipping snake tendrils, she ran toward the seemingly tiny circle of light she knew was the mouth of the cave, beyond which lay the sea.

Denied their first choice from the dinner menu, the serpents all began to converge on Pan, who hovered in the air in their midst.

While he had been wildly flailing away at them, though, Pan had noticed the vipers had recoiled more violently from his torch than from his dagger. Accustomed to dwelling in near total darkness deep within the cave, the snakes were sensitive to the point of pain to the presence of light.

Still hovering, Pan began to spin round and round. The torch and its light circled with him; and though they hissed and snapped, the vipers still recoiled away from him.

Seeing an opening, Pan shot out from their midst, flying in the direction

Alice had run. When he caught up with her, he landed and began running alongside her.

"Faster!" he urged her. "They're coming after us!"

"I'm running as fast as I can!" Alice gasped, and so she truly thought. But when the hissing sounds of the snakes behind them drew closer, she discovered she was indeed capable of even more speed.

The mouth of the cave lay tantalizingly close just ahead of them, but now she could feel hot breath expelled by the pursuing serpents dancing across the back of her neck. The sound of the waves crashing against the rocks at the entrance to the cave drowned out the noise of the vipers, but Alice was sure their dripping fangs were poised to sink into her pale flesh.

Bursting out of the cave and into daylight, Pan again took to flight, grabbing Alice's arm and carrying her up with him. As he did so, he tossed his sputtering torch back over his shoulder in the desperate hope that it would deter the serpents until he and Alice could reach safety.

Alice heard deadly jaws snap tightly closed behind her. Something tugged at the hem of her dress, threatening to yank her out of Pan's grasp. She cried out as she felt herself being pulled away from Pan and toward the waiting gullet of one of the vile snakes. The boy tightened his hold on her and managed to jerk her free with a tearing of cloth.

Loud, agonized shrieks of pain ripped the air. Both Pan and Alice dared to look back over their shoulders. Several of the serpents, desirous of catching and swallowing their prey, had recklessly lunged out beyond the mouth of their cavernous lair.

They paid a scorching price for their foolishness. The bright sunlight that served to hold them captive within the depths of the earth now struck them full on. The vipers writhed in pain as the sun seared their slimy hides. Puffs of smoke and a smell like burnt pork rose from them. Wailing like banshees, they retreated back into the eternal shadows.

Pan appeared to be somewhat strained by the time he made it back to Marooner's Rock with Alice and the chest in tow. Touching down, both children fell to their knees, panting for breath.

Millisandra the mermaid, who had been anxiously awaiting their return, was somewhat breathless herself from the horrifying glimpses she had caught of the monstrous serpents inside the cave. Such was her relief that she threw her arms around Peter and hugged him tightly.

"No one else had ever entered that cave and made it back out alive," she gasped, "and now I know why!" She squeezed Pan tighter.

"You'll be even *more* admired by my people now, Peter!"

"*I* went into the cave, too, remember?" Alice snorted somewhat resentfully.

"Of *course* you did, little girl," Millisandra sniffed. "And Peter brought you out!"

"That's not important right now," Pan interrupted, feeling suddenly uncomfortable. He reached out and took the nearly forgotten chest from Alice's hands.

Flipping the latch that held it closed, he opened the lid. As he had been told to expect, inside it was another rolled scroll, lying atop a plush velvet cushion. He handed the scroll to Alice, who unfurled it and read the message it contained aloud.

Flesh covers bone, save when bone becomes stone,
And the biggest of all is the one that's alone.
With eyes that don't see and a mouth that can't speak,
Yet you'll see and you'll hear how to find what you seek.

Alice's eyes lit up. "Since we found the chest right where the first riddle led us, and since it did indeed hold the next riddle…why, that would seem to make it more likely that there really *is* a treasure!"

She couldn't help but notice that Pan did not seem to be nearly as thrilled and enthusiastic as was she.

"What's wrong, Peter?" she asked.

"I think I've already solved the riddle," he said glumly. His expression made Alice feel a sense of dread.

"What is it?" she asked, and Pan frowned.

"It's directing us to go to *Skull Rock*."

Chapter 11

*P*an was clearly not happy as he tightened the final rope that bound half a dozen long, bamboo shoots together; putting the finishing touches to a simple raft he was constructing.

Sitting on the nearby sand, Alice continued to weave together the palm fronds that would serve as the raft's sail.

"Tell me again," she said, "why we can't simply *fly* out to this rock you talk about."

"And again," he growled, "the answer is the same as before. You are too heavy for me to carry that far."

"Are you saying I'm *fat*?" she accused.

"I'm saying I can only carry so much weight," he replied.

"Nor would I need to," he groused, "if you would just fly on your own!"

"I've told you," Alice snapped back, "I can't!"

"You could if you believed you could."

"I've tried," Alice deflected. "But it's impossible!"

"How can it be impossible, girl? You've seen *me* fly!"

"But that's *you*—not *me*!"

"It's because you refuse to be a child," Pan accused. "You don't want to be free."

"Can't one be free—*and* a grown-up?"

"Have *you* ever known a grown-up that was free?" Pan asked.

Alice's face scrunched up in concentration. "I admit that at the moment I can't think of one. But it still seems to me that you could simply *teach* me how to fly!"

In response to this, Peter's face looked almost saddened. "To do that," he said, "I would first have to teach you to be free." He sighed deeply.

"I don't think anyone can do that."

"What do you mean?" Alice asked, stung by his words.

"I think you've worked so long and so hard to become a proper lady, Alice…that I'm afraid you've forgotten how to just be *happy*. Happy for no reason; happy just to be alive.

"You can't be unhappy and be a child. You can't be unhappy and be free. You can't be unhappy and fly."

Alice had no response for that, so she silently bent back over her work. "The sail is ready, I think," she said at last.

"Then we'd best cast off," Pan replied softly.

He pushed the raft into the sea before he and Alice hopped aboard it. Pan picked up a flat piece of wood that would serve as both oar and rudder while Alice unfurled her makeshift sail.

The westerly winds filled the sail and the raft fairly flew across the mostly smooth waters. Pan adjusted his tiller to set a course that took them slightly north of true west.

Pan had described their destination for Alice the previous evening, but no mere words could have prepared Alice for the sight that met her eyes within two hours of the duo setting sail.

It was a small island, virtually devoid of vegetation and therefore of much noticeable life. Three-fourths of the space inside its shorelines was occupied by a single, large hill rising some thirty feet into the sky.

The hill had the appearance of being one enormous and bare rock—which even larger hands had chiseled and shaped in the likeness of a human skull that had been stripped of all flesh and muscle (hence the name "Skull Rock"). This appearance was amplified by a series of depressions and caves located approximately where eye and nose sockets would be on an actual skull of that size. Its "mouth" was the largest of the caverns, set near the ground.

"According to local legend," Pan said as they drew closer to the depressing shore, "two giants once fought each other here."

"Why did they fight?" Alice asked.

"The legends don't say. Maybe it was just because that's what giants do. Their battle raged for months and their struggles stirred up waves a hundred feet high.

"This battle didn't end until one of the giants was dead. The winner cut off his head and left the skull atop this island to serve as a testament to his great victory and to warn anyone else who might dare to challenge him."

"You don't *believe* such fables, do you?" Alice asked.

"No more than I believe girls can travel through mirrors," Pan replied mischievously.

They experienced no difficulties in reaching Skull Rock and Alice found herself thinking that if it were not for the serious nature of their journey it would have been quite a pleasant voyage.

That pleasure diminished the closer they got to the island. Though she knew in her mind that it was likely only an accident of nature that had left a promontory looking so disturbingly like a giant skull, it was also her mind that conjured up thoughts of headless behemoths and made her shiver.

Beaching their small but sturdy craft, lowering its palm frond sail and tethering it to a rock, Pan and Alice began the short walk to the base of Skull Rock.

"*Coooome*," a deep and mournful voice seemed to wail at them, beckoning to them.

"Oh my goodness!" Alice cried, crouching down behind a small boulder. "What was *that*, Peter? Peter?"

She looked over her shoulder and saw that Pan had backed away from her by several yards.

"Are you planning to run away?" she asked incredulously.

"Me?" he snorted. "Don't be silly! I was—I was only backing up so I could see the skull more fully."

"*Coooome*," the voice moaned once again. It was now plain the cry was issuing out of the mouth of Skull Rock.

Alice cocked her head to one side. "Do you suppose it's possible that isn't a voice at all? That it's only the *wind* howling through the mouth of the cave at its base?"

"That is *exactly* what I was thinking," Pan declared. "Come on, let's check it out."

Alice was content to let Pan lead the way. Seeing that he kept his hand on the hilt of his dagger gave her at least small comfort; he had made good use of its blade against that nest of giant vipers.

But would even the sharpest steel protect them from *ghosts*?

Luckily, the cave that gave the appearance of being the "mouth" of the giant skull did not extend very far back into the hill; there was nothing on the little island from which they could have fashioned a suitable torch.

"*Coooome*," the eerie voice seemed to call them in and the two children followed.

Right into the path of a flock of screeching *bats*!

Chapter 12

lice shrieked and threw her hands up in front of her face. Leathery wings slapped at her and taloned feet caught in and pulled painfully at her hair.

She dropped to her knees and felt Pan do likewise, covering her body with his own as the bats flew around them. At last the final member of the swarm fluttered past and on its way to wherever it is that bats go when they have been disturbed.

"Rats with wings!" Pan spat. "I hate them!"

"Are they gone?" Alice asked before daring to rise from her knees.

"For now," Pan replied, offering a hand to help her to her feet.

"You look a fright," Alice said. "And I'm sure I do, too!"

"Then maybe any ghosts we encounter will be scared of *us*!" Pan declared, throwing his head back and laughing.

He really was a rather remarkable lad, Alice thought, for all his cockiness and sometimes irritating boy ways. She'd certainly never met anyone else quite like him.

She wished she'd had him beside her during her maddening trips to Wonderland—whether they were only dreams or not. Perhaps, she pondered, she had merely been too young back then to have dreamed of a boy like Peter Pan.

As they stepped into the confines of the cave, they were met by a warm, outgoing breeze. Doubtless it was this rushing of air coming out of the cavern that created the noise that sounded like a mournful voice.

"The wind appears to be coming through here," Pan observed, finding a small opening in the back wall of the cave.

It didn't take long for them to thoroughly examine all sides of the cave, including its ceiling; but the search revealed no sign of what they expected and hoped to find: yet another chest containing yet another riddle.

"That still leaves three other possibilities," Pan said.

"The nose and the eyes of the skull," Alice replied.

Pan led the way back out of the cave and spent a few moments staring up at the face of the cliff before him. It did not appear to be too steep an incline, so he began to climb. Alice came right behind him.

The depression that created the illusion of being a nasal cavity was even shallower than the cave below and a search of it quickly yielded the same results. So they continued their climb up to the nearest of the eye sockets.

Only upon entering it could they see there was a hole in one wall, connecting it to the other socket so it almost formed a single cavern.

Alice had taken several steps into the cavern before realizing yet again that Pan was not beside her. Turning around, she saw that he was still standing at the entrance to this cavern. Hands on hips, his back to her, he appeared to be staring intently to the west, away from the island.

"Is everything all right, Peter?" she asked of him.

"I suppose," he said rather absently, turning back toward her. "Now, let's find us a chest!"

Knowing this was the only place remaining where they might hope to find the box, they were painstaking and meticulous in their search.

"Peter!" Alice cried out just as it was beginning to seem hopeless. "I may have found it!"

Pan rushed to her side. He had to squint closely and feel about with his hands, but he was at last just able to make out what did appear to be part of a manmade, squared object projecting from the wall of the cave a few feet above the ground.

When he grabbed hold of it and tried to pull it forward, it budged not an inch, nor even a fraction of an inch.

Hoping to get a better look at the object and what was holding it captive, Pan used his strike-a-light to send a small shower of sparks its way.

The sparks burned out in seconds, but in that brief flare of light Pan and Alice could discern the problem. The chest was partially embedded inside the cave's back wall! It looked almost as if the stone had briefly melted, oozed over the box and then froze back into solid rock hardness, gripping the chest in an unbreakable hold.

"What do we do?" Alice asked. "We have no digging tools and by the time we might could find some—poor Tink could be dead!"

"We just have to want it more than the rock does," Pan said stubbornly.

He slowly floated up and above the part of the chest that was visible and pressed his back against the cavern wall holding it.

"Take hold of the chest with both hands, one on either side of it," he directed Alice, who did so at once.

"When I give the word, lift both feet off the ground so that all your weight will be on the chest." Alice nodded.

"Now!" Pan cried.

Alice did as instructed, lifting her feet and pulling downward with all her might. As the same time, from above, Pan braced his back against the cave's wall and ceiling and pushed down on the chest with both feet.

They pushed and they pulled until Alice's fingers gave way and her feet dropped back to the cavern floor. She took a step back, panting heavily.

"Again!" Pan urged. "We can do it—I know we can!"

Alice was not quite so certain as he was, but she gamely gave it another go. As she pressed down on the chest with every ounce of her strength, she was momentarily appalled to realize that in her efforts she was *grunting* in a most unladylike manner.

Similar sounds were issuing from the straining Pan, though, so she thought it unlikely that he would notice this lapse in decorum.

Just as she was about to admit defeat, she heard a sound something like that made by a tree when its roots were being torn from the hands of Mother Earth. Bits of dislodged stone trickled down the cave wall.

"It's *moving*, Peter!" she cried.

"Don't stop," he admonished. "Keep pulling!"

Neither child was prepared or properly braced when the chest abruptly tore free from its stone dungeon. With nothing to stop her, Alice fell flat on the floor of the cave.

And with nothing to stop him, Pan fell flat on top of her!

Alice coughed and waved one hand like a fan to dissipate the choking dust that swirled about her. As it did, she found herself looking straight up into the dirt-smudged, smiling face of Pan.

"Do you *mind*?" she said with less indignation than she perhaps should have felt.

"Not at all!" he replied, laughing in that joyful way of his.

"Get off!" she scolded, bucking him off and sending him rolling across the floor of the cave. He quickly sat up, smiling and resting his elbows on his knees.

"That was kind of fun!" he chirped.

"It was kind of *filthy*!" Alice rebuked, slapping at the dust coating her dress: a garment that had been oh so clean and nice just a few days ago but was quickly becoming little more than a dirty and tattered rag.

"Fun often *is*!" Pan declared, leaping nimbly to his feet.

He was very nearly knocked back off them by a wind close to gale force that now sprang up and roared into the cavern. It funneled into the large hole that now gaped where the chest had been embedded in the cave wall.

The horizontal column of air rushed downward and was expelled out the cavern below that formed the "mouth" of Skull Rock. As it did, the sound as of an anguished moaning coming out of that mouth grew louder and more intense.

"I have a feeling we should get out of here as quick as we can," Alice said, practically yelling to be heard over the roaring wind.

"Let's try following the wind," Pan suggested, pointing to the hole in the back wall. "That might be safer than trying to climb back down the open face in this bluster!"

Alice heartily agreed and they clambered through the hole. The passageway leading down to the base of the skull was wide enough to accommodate them yet sloped enough that there was little fear of falling.

As the two of them raced out of the mouth of the skull, they ran smack-on into even heavier winds. They bent into it and slowly pushed their way forward.

"What's that sound?" Alice shouted.

"It's called wind!" Pan replied.

"Not *that* sound—the *other* sound!"

Pan heard it too now. A low rumbling that was rapidly growing louder. He looked down at his feet and saw small pebbles seeming to dance up and down.

Then the very ground itself heaved upward like an ocean wave, nearly throwing the two children off their feet.

"*Earthquake!*" Pan shouted.

Chapter 13

his whole island could sink beneath us," Pan said frantically. "And that's if it doesn't *swallow* us first!"

"We've got to get to the raft!" Alice cried.

The distance they had to travel was not far but it was treacherous. The ground buckled and tossed beneath them like a wild stallion.

As they neared the moored raft, the rocky outcropping upon which it was tied cracked and fell into the sea. Untethered, the raft began to float away rapidly.

Without hesitation, Pan grabbed Alice under her arms and leaped into the air, flying them the short way out to the raft. As he reached for the tiller, he saw Alice trying to raise the sail.

"Forget the sail!" he called to her. "The wind is against us!"

Nodding, she ran back to help him with the tiller. She used only one hand, for she was using the other one to keep the chest tightly tucked in the bend of her arm.

The two of them would have made any seasoned seaman proud with the way they handled their light craft, skillfully maneuvering it between, up and down swells in the ocean.

The raft nearly capsized, though, when a sudden spray of water, almost like an exploding geyser, shot up alongside it.

"Good heavens!" Alice cried, her eyes growing wider. Something was rising up from the depths, right in the middle of the geyser.

A *hand* broke the surface of the water. Not an ordinary hand; this one was composed only of *bones*—and was nearly as large as the tree house in which Pan lived.

A skeletal arm was attached to the hand—and the arm in turn was attached to an entire, great, skeletal body!

But not *quite* entire. The giant, animated skeleton was complete save in one very important detail.

It had no *head*.

So tall was this behemoth that when it rose to its full height (less the height of a head, naturally), the waters of the sea came up only to slightly above his bony knees.

Thrashing about blindly, the giant stirred the waters up even more fiercely. Caught in its wake, the raft began to pitch madly.

Thinking desperately, Alice thrust the chest into Pan's hands.

"Fly away, Peter," she urged. "I'll try to keep the raft afloat and follow you as best I can!"

Pan recoiled as if it was a red-hot coal she was attempting to hand him. The girl persisted, though, and at last he accepted it. With a hop and a skip he launched himself off the raft and into the darkly billowing sky.

Left alone, Alice threw all her weight against the tiller in an effort to steer it clear from the worst of the turbulence threatening to capsize it.

As the raft rose up on a swelling wave, she glanced upward and was surprised to see Pan a short distance away; he was merely hovering motionless in the air with his back to her. He then spun and dived back down to the raft.

"I can't let one friend die to save another!" he shouted, adding his weight to Alice's to control the rudder. She smiled, wiped a spray of water away from her face and again put her back to it.

Waving its arms about blindly, the giant skeleton slowly moved past their position, heading in the general direction of the island. Even though it had no ears (since it had no head), it still seemed to be drawn toward the howling sounds still issuing forth from the mouth of Skull Rock.

The skeletal giant did not stop until he bumped into the edge of the small island. With a sound akin to that of a thousand rusty hinges, he bent over and began to blindly grope about with his hands.

When a giant thumb poked into one of the eye sockets of the enormous rock skull, the colossus softly ran his hands over its surface. Taking hold on either side of the skull, the giant began to carefully pull upward. If he exerted too much pressure, he risked crushing the skull into a gigantic pile of gravel; not enough and the skull would remain securely attached to the island.

"*Aaaaaahh!*" A sound like an enormous sigh of relief whooshed out of the mouth of the skull as it was pulled loose and lifted into the air.

Raising it high, the skeletal giant then set the head atop its spinal column. He had neglected to turn the skull as he lifted it, however—so the head, while back atop his body, was facing *backwards*!

Reaching up to again take hold of the skull, the giant firmly turned it right way round amidst a teeth-grinding, scraping sound.

Satisfied that its body was now as whole as it would ever again be, the giant sidestepped what little remained of the island and resumed walking. It continued onward, the seawater rising higher and higher around it, until its entire, giant frame was swallowed up and reclaimed by the waters.

"That sound we heard while we were sailing to the island," Alice speculated. "It wasn't calling to *us*. The skull must have been trying to let the body know where to find it."

"Yes," Pan said. "Only the call wasn't loud enough for the body to hear under the water—until we dislodged the chest. That's when the sound grew louder and led the body right to the skull!"

"I think that's a good thing," Alice said. "A body really *should* have a head. Don't you agree, Peter?"

"I do indeed, Alice."

As the skeletal giant dropped from sight beneath the waves, the wind fell to nearly nothing and the rolling sea subsided. The way was clear now for Alice and Pan to set a course and sail without further difficulty back to the mainland.

The evening of that day found the two of them well inland, enjoying the comforts of a roaring fire. They stood as close to it as they dared, turning back and forth like guinea hens on a spit so that their drenched clothing might dry. Afterwards, they enjoyed a sparse and simple but welcome dinner together.

"I'm not sure I properly thanked you, Peter," Alice said at last. "For coming back for me today, I mean."

Pan gave an exaggerated shrug. "What else could I do? Without you—I couldn't read the next riddle."

"Oh, yes. Of course." If the boy detected the disappointment in Alice's voice, he pretended not to.

"I guess we'd better get to it, then," she said, lifting the chest up and setting it in her lap. She opened it, withdrew the now expected scroll and read aloud the words written upon it.

Look you now for the hole in the clouds,
And a stairway to the stars.
Three there be, though only two can you see,
And the other roars aloud.

"I don't know why whoever hid this big treasure didn't simply draw a *map* showing its location," Alice said.

"Even if he had," Pan mused, "he probably would have cut it into separate pieces that would have to be reassembled."

"I suppose you're right. Do you have any idea who he was—the person who hid the treasure and wrote the riddles?"

"No. I didn't even know there *was* a treasure until that wicked woman told us about it."

"I'm surprised you didn't know all about it, Peter. You seem to know *everything* about Neverland."

Pan poked at the fire with a stick before answering. "Not everything, obviously. I didn't know about that headless giant living under the sea, for instance."

"Well, I don't suppose it's really possible for anyone to know everything."

"No," he replied glumly. But it's often the things you don't know that get you killed!"

"A BODY REALLY SHOULD HAVE A HEAD."

Alice did not care to think about things such as this. "Have you put your brain to work on solving the riddle yet?"

"I sort of suspected what the answer would be even before you read the riddle," Pan said to her surprise.

"How could you have?"

"Remember when I stood staring to the west out of the eye of Skull Rock?"

"Yes."

"Well, from there I could just make out the place we have to go next."

"And where might that be?"

Pan tossed his stick into the fire and looked up into the clear night sky before answering her.

"*The Misty Mountains.*"

Chapter 14

Not long after the sun rose the next day, the two children set out for their next destination.

The most straightway course to that location took them through the middle of a dense forest.

Every tree in it was taller than Alice's house and they grew so close together that their limbs very nearly blotted out the sun.

"What sort of animals are there hereabouts?" Alice asked at one point. Various growls and roars, while not near at hand, were still plainly heard enough to be somewhat disconcerting.

"Just the usual," Pan said cavalierly. "Wolves and bears, mostly. Perhaps the occasional tiger."

"Oh, my!"

A loud screech caused Alice to jump and cry out. If pushed to describe it, she would have said it sounded the way she would have imagined a vulture would sound if its tail feathers were caught in a thrashing machine.

"What on earth was that?" she asked.

"Just a Neverbird."

"I've never heard of a Neverbird!"

"I'm not surprised. After all, you'd never heard of Never*land*, either."

"That's true." She craned her head back in hopes of catching a glimpse at the creature.

"Are they dangerous?"

"I suppose so—if you happen to be a worm."

Alice giggled slightly at that, but then gulped as she heard yet again the distant roar of a beast she was quite certain was more formidable than a Neverbird.

"This *is* a bit of a scary place, don't you think?"

"No scarier than Kensington Square," Pan replied.

Alice stopped in her tracks. "You know about Kensington?"

"I know it very well," Pan said, to her surprise. "I was born not far from there. I still visit it from time to time, when I have nothing better to do." He graced Alice with a smile.

"That's where I first saw *you*, Alice."

Now the girl was more than surprised; she was astounded. "You saw *me*? When?"

"Oh, I don't pay much mind to one day or another," Pan said. (Or week or year, for that matter!)

"But I'm sure it was just before you showed up in Neverland."

Alice gasped. "So *that's* why I felt like somebody was watching me that day!"

"Really?" Pan said. "How odd; because I felt that someone was watching *me* that day!"

"So, somebody was watching you watching me?"

"I don't know. Maybe."

"But why were *you* watching *me*?" Alice asked. The whole thing was becoming a bit confusing to her.

"I didn't say I was *watching* you," Pan replied impatiently. "I said I *saw* you."

"Well, isn't that the same thing, really?"

"Not at all. I saw lots of people there. You were just one of them."

"But of all the people you must have seen that day—you remember me specifically?"

"I wouldn't say specifically. If one of those others had dropped down in the middle of our fairy party—I probably would have remembered them, too."

"Are you sure?"

"I can't be absolutely sure, I suppose—since no one other than you *did* drop in on our party. But I'm pretty sure."

"I'm not sure I'm sure of anything anymore!" Alice moaned.

"Maybe you should just do what I do when I'm not sure," Pan suggested. "Play make believe!"

"Ohh, I'm not sure what I believe anymore, either."

"Then, see? That puts you half way to make believe already!"

Alice *was* sure her head was beginning to ache from all this and she held it in her hands and shook it slightly.

"Tell me again," she finally said. "Why were you in Kensington?"

"I told you. I was born near there."

"So London is your home?"

"It was once; only for a moment. But that's another story."

"I'd like to hear it."

"Are you sure?"

"Absolutely," Alice urged.

"Very well." If nothing else, Pan thought, engaging Alice in conversation had at least momentarily distracted her from all the things that made the forest frightening.

"I was only a day old," he began. "Lying in my crib, and quite content to be doing so. Minding my own business, you might say.

"Then mother and father decided to come and stand over me, without so much as a by your leave.

"If that wasn't bad enough, they then began to discuss my future: what sort of schools I would attend, what profession I might pursue when I grew up. What sort of girl I might marry.

"Well, let me tell you; I wanted nothing to do with any of this nonsense. Especially the part about growing up.

"So, that very night—I ran away from home!"

Pan smiled rather smugly; right proud of himself, he was. But then he saw Alice frowning and giving her head a bit of a shake.

"What?" he asked her.

"Well…I'm sorry to say this, Peter," Alice replied, trying her very utmost best to be polite and diplomatic, "but that story of yours simply can't be *true*."

"And why not?" he huffed.

"It's simple, really. In the first place, a newborn baby wouldn't possibly be able to understand what two grown-ups were saying." Pan merely stared at Alice, so she continued on.

"And in the second place, even if he could understand them—he couldn't *crawl* away, let alone *run* away!"

"I would think," Pan finally responded, "that by now you would have realized that I am a most exceptional boy!"

Alice tried unsuccessfully to stifle a giggle.

"The point is," Pan continued in an icy tone, "that one can get along just fine without a mother and father."

"That's a *horrible* thing to say!" Alice shouted. But the shout quickly became a sob.

Tears flowed freely and Alice buried her face in her cupped hands. The pain from the recent loss of her own parents was still too fresh, too overwhelming. She had told Pan of their passing, but in the heat of the moment he had forgotten.

Peter, alas, lacked the ability to bring comfort to her in her sorrow and instead made things worse.

"You seem to be doing just fine without parents," he said thoughtlessly. "For a girl, I mean."

"To use your own words," she hissed at him through clenched teeth, "that's not the point. The point is that I loved them and they loved me—and now they're gone forever!"

A fresh round of crying began then, and this time Pan was smart enough to say nothing. When the tears at last subsided and Alice had wiped her face dry, she looked at him with pity.

"Don't you love *your* parents, Peter?"

"Of course I do!"

"And don't they love you?"

"Of course they do—did—do!"

"You don't seem quite sure," Alice said skeptically.

"I could tell you things about my parents," Pan said defensively.

"I wish you would," she prompted.

"Take my father, for instance. He was a soldier. A great one. A hero. But he was killed in the war."

"Which war was that?"

"The big one," Pan said vaguely.

"I'm very sorry to hear that," Alice said with great sympathy. (Being a girl, she was much better about such things than was a boy, especially a boy like Pan.)

"And what of your mother? Is she still alive?"

"Maybe."

"*Maybe?*" This time, Alice was unable to completely contain herself. "Don't you *know?*"

Alice didn't need to be an adult to see that her words had stung Pan and made him angry.

"She was the best mother of all!" he asserted strongly. "And the most beautiful. And she gave me lots of kisses when I was a baby." He leaped to his feet, glaring down at Alice.

"But I still say grown-ups are a nuisance—and are best lived without!"

Alice jumped up, growing angry herself. "And *I* say you don't know what you're talking about, Mr. Pan!"

"Oh, no?"

"No!"

"Children really shouldn't fight, I must say," a slightly high pitched voice said from above, causing both of them to jump in surprise.

"They're not very good at it."

Pan and Alice stared tensely about, seeking the source of the voice. Pan's right hand hovered just above the hilt of his sheathed dagger.

"Look!" he cried, pointing to one of the lower branches of a nearby tree.

Sure enough, seeming to float in the air just above that branch, could be seen a wide, disembodied *mouth*, its large white teeth flashing in a big, broad grin.

"I *know* that mouth!" Alice exclaimed.

"You know a mouth?" Peter said.

"What I mean to say is that I know to whom that mouth is attached. I think." She peered upward more intently.

"Can that possibly be *you*?" she said tentatively. "Is it *Cheshire Cat*?"

That's *precisely* who it was. As the two children watched in awe, the head and body of a large, pudgy, striped cat now came into view behind and around the toothy mouth that had spoken to them.

Alice had previously made the acquaintance of this remarkable feline—which had the ability to appear and disappear at will—on one of her trips to Wonderland. This seemed to present further proof that those sojourns had not been mere dreams at all, as Alice had been assured by her family—but real.

"What are *you* doing here, Cheshire?" Alice asked of him.

"Well, I have to be *somewhere*, now don't I?" the feline replied. "And being a cat—I can go anywhere I please."

"Well, I'm pleased that it pleases you to be here," Alice said, greeting him with a curtsy. "You were one of my very favorite things about Wonderland."

"Naturally—because I'm a cat."

"I am indeed fond of cats," Alice admitted. "When I was much younger, I owned a cat named *Dinah*. She was a lovely creatures."

"You did *what*?" Cheshire demanded, the tawny fur on its arching back rising slightly.

"I said I once owned a cat—"

"You most certainly did *not*!" Cheshire's voice grew harsh.

"I most certainly *did*!" Alice snapped back, scowling at him.

"My dear child," Cheshire purred. "Do you know what you call a cat that allows itself to be *owned*?"

"What?"

"A *dog*!"

"Cats, dogs—what difference does it make?" Pan suddenly barked, interrupting their hot exchange.

"We're wasting time, which is something my friend Tinker Bell—who is neither a dog *nor* a cat—has precious little of!"

"I'm sorry, Peter," Alice said contritely. "You're right, of course." She turned her eyes up toward the still grinning feline.

"The two of us are on a very important, quest, Cheshire. Would you care to join us?"

"I thank you for the invitation, Miss," the cat replied graciously. "But since I've only just arrived here, I really would like some time to myself, to go exploring."

"I understand," Alice said. Even as she spoke, she saw that the odd fellow was beginning to disappear again. Already, she could see right through parts of him.

"Besides," he added in a stage whisper, motioning with his head, "I don't think he (meaning Peter) much likes cats."

"Why ever wouldn't he?" Alice asked with conviction.

"Well, you know what they say," Cheshire told her as he continued to fade from view.

"Some people are cat people..." There was nothing left to be seen of Cheshire now save for that wide and slightly disconcerting grin.

"And some people are stupid!"

Then, even his smile disappeared.

Chapter 15

*P*an wasted no time in pressing on toward the next destination in their treasure hunt. He set a brisk pace, but Alice gamely kept up with him stride for stride with nary a complaint. Part of her mind, however, remained on what they had recently left behind.

"However do you think it came to pass that the giant we encountered lost his head?" she asked Pan.

"Given how highly eager he was to retrieve it, I think it's safe to say it's unlikely he beheaded himself! And why did he pick that precise moment to go looking for it?"

"As I think I told you," Pan replied, "the legend is that it was a *second* giant who did the beheading."

"But why, I wonder," Alice continued. "Surely one doesn't go around lopping off heads for no good reason!"

"As to that, I couldn't say," Pan replied. "But then, not being a giant myself, I have no idea why a giant might do *anything*!"

"I see your point," Alice said. "But given that the body rose up out of the sea right after we laid our hands on the riddle box—do you think one is connected to the other?"

"It's possible, I suppose," Pan admitted.

Having jumped aboard this particular train of thought, Alice was determined to ride it to the end of the tracks.

"And why do you suppose, once he got his head on straight, he took off for the open sea? Where could he have been going?"

"Again, I can't say for sure, Alice. To another island, maybe. Maybe he's gone in search of the other giant, in hopes of a rematch!"

"That certainly sounds plausible," Alice said. "In which case, he should be far, far away from us by now." A new thought made her brow furrow.

"Uh-oh," she murmured.

"What?"

"What if he isn't moving *toward* the other giant—assuming there *is* another giant—but instead is fleeing to get *away* from him?"

"What if he is?"

"Well, if another giant is chasing him—that could put *us* right in its path!"

Pan stopped dead in his tracks to consider that possibility.

"I'm fairly certain that's not the case," he said at last. "Surely if there was a giant—skeletal or otherwise—roaming willy-nilly around Neverland, I'd have seen or heard of him before now!"

"Oh? So, does that mean you know *all* there is to know about what there is in Neverland?" Alice challenged

"Yes and no," Pan replied vaguely, wiggling one hand back and forth.

"Yes and no? What does *that* mean?"

Pan tried to assure Alice that he was neither being a smart aleck nor intentionally misleading in his response.

"I've traveled far and wide over Neverland," he told her, "and one thing you should know about it—is that it *changes*."

"What exactly do you mean, it changes?" Alice was growing more, not less, enlightened by this conversation.

"I can't really explain it," Pan admitted. "I can only describe it. From time to time, the size and shape of Neverland changes: not a lot, but a little. It *mostly* stays the same, but sometimes places and things that weren't there before just sort of pop up. Or pop out." He scratched his head, dislodging a flower.

"Now that I think of it, that might be why no new Lost Boys have shown up here for a while now." He looked at Alice, and (even though, quite frankly, when it came to girls Peter was not the most observant of boys) saw that she had a skeptical look on her face.

"I'm sorry," said she, "but while I haven't studied a great deal of geography, I find it hard to believe that such a thing is possible."

"Oh?" Pan scoffed. "Tell me, Alice; just how many *im*possible things will you have to see before you admit that *anything* is possible?"

Alice squinted at him through one eye. "I suppose you make a good argument. But is there anything here that *doesn't* change?"

"Lots of things!" Pan replied. "At least that I know of. Lots and lots of places." He smiled.

"And my truly best friends haven't come and gone. Truly best friends never do."

"I suppose that's true…er, truly," Alice concurred.

"You must have lots of friends waiting for you back in the Real World," Pan said.

It was an innocent enough statement. Yet it caused Alice considerably more pain that she would have expected—or than Pan could possibly have known it would.

For the sobering fact was that Alice wasn't sure if she had *any* truly best friends!

"I get along just fine with the girls and boys I go to school with," she told Pan. "But I seldom socialize with any of them outside the schoolyard. I never really gave it much thought before, but it seems I spend more time alone with my imagination than I do with other children."

"That's not entirely bad," Pan consoled her. "At least as long as you're young. Imagination—along with laughter—seems to grow more elusive as one ages."

"My sister Elsbeth is my friend," Alice continued ruminating. "But she became less so after she grew up—and even less so after she got married."

("Will she become more or even less of a friend if I come live with her?" Alice wondered. "Or if I too get married?")

"I loved my parents, of course," she went on aloud. "But I suppose you can't really be both a parent *and* a friend at the same time." Her forehead furrowed.

"Maybe that's why my mind created Wonderland," she said (though by now she was beginning to believe that it was a very real place after all).

"So that at least in my dreams I could have some company." She frowned. "I must say, though, that with the exception of Cheshire Cat, I didn't consider most of the creatures I met there to be friends either."

"As to whether Wonderland is real or not, I can't say," Peter told her, "never having been there myself. But what you've said sounds rather…sad."

"Yes, I suppose it does. Yes. It does." The next thought struck Alice like a physical blow.

"I guess—I guess that means I'm an unlikable person!"

"You certainly *can* be," Pan agreed far too quickly.

"Well, the same just *might* be said of *you*!" Alice fired back angrily.

Rather than growing peeved himself, Pan surprised her by smiling. "*Everybody's* unlikable some of the time," he philosophized.

"But that's usually not a problem—unless you're unlikable *most* of the time!"

"And what if you're unlikable *all* of the time?" Alice asked.

Pan held his hands out, palms up. "That depends. If you're *poor* and unlikable, you have *no* friends.

"But if you're *rich* and unlikable—you have *lots* of friends!"

"That's a terrible thought and it doesn't seem fair at all—but you may be right." Alice's voice grew even sadder. "I must be poorer than I thought."

"Don't be silly!" Pan replied, hoping to brighten the girl's mood. "Just look at all the friends you've made here in Neverland in just a few days!"

"What friends?" she said skeptically.

"*Me*, for one," Pan said sincerely.

"And don't forget Tink. And believe you me, that's saying a lot; she doesn't warm up to just anybody. In fact, much as it pains me to admit it—she can be downright *hateful*!"

"Yet you still like her," Alice observed, slightly baffled.

"Why wouldn't I? After all—she's seldom mean to *me*!"

"Still," Alice said, "it sounds like being a friend can be awfully difficult."

"Maybe that's why you feel like you don't have any," Pan speculated. "Maybe, back in the Real World, you just haven't found many others who are *worth* the trouble!"

"Perhaps," Alice said pensively. "Or maybe none of them thought *I* was worth the trouble."

"Maybe so," Pan conceded. "But I don't think *any*body is friends with *every*body. And it's better to have just one *good* friend than it is to have a hundred acquaintances."

"That sounds very wise, Mister Pan," Alice joked. "Hearing those words, one might almost mistake you for a real grown-up."

"Bite your tongue! Despite what some people may think, age and wisdom don't necessarily go hand-in-hand."

"That may be why they say there's no fool like an old fool," Alice remarked.

"One more reason not to grow old," Pan asserted, then poked himself in the chest with one thumb.

"Just stick with me, little Alice. By the time this adventure is finished—you'll have lots of friends!"

Alice laughed brightly. "Then by all means—let's continue!"

Chapter 16

Late that afternoon (nearer to evening, actually), Pan called a temporary halt to their trek as he and Alice emerged from the woods to find themselves at the edge of a very broad meadow.

The soil hereabouts must have been rich and fertile, for they could see many acres had been prepared and planted with a variety of crops. A clean, clear brook meandered through it; and on either side of the stream sat a dozen or more small huts, with stucco walls and thatched roofs.

"We talked about places with which I was unfamiliar," Pan said. "Well, this is one of them. So we'd best keep an eye on it before we approach any closer; try to determine whether or not its people are hostile to new arrivals."

"The only people I see at all," Alice observed, "appear to be children, based on their size. That seems a little odd."

"Maybe all the adults are indoors," Pan said. "Or working the fields. Or off hunting."

"Maybe."

"One sure way to find out, I suppose," Pan declared boldly as he began to walk toward the small village. Alice rolled her eyes, but stepped forward right beside him.

By the time they were halfway there, any fears of being met with hostility were assuaged. Upon spying the two advancing strangers, the villagers shrieked as in terror and rushed into their simple huts. There was not a person in sight as Pan and Alice strolled into the middle of the enclave.

"Hello!" Pan called loudly. He received no response.

"They seem to be afraid of us," Alice said.

"I wonder why?" Pan pondered.

"We're friends," Alice called out. "Really. We don't mean any harm."

They could hear hushed but frantic murmuring coming from inside some of the huts. Finally, the door of one of them slowly opened and a small figure clutching a short shepherd's crook stepped out.

"Oh, my goodness!" Alice exclaimed softly as she got a better look at this lone brave soul.

Although he was no taller than a typical five-year-old child was, he was a fully developed adult! Proof of this could be seen in his face, which was lightly bearded and showed the wear and wrinkles of a man who had spent a lifetime in the out of doors.

"Hello," Alice said, smiling as she curtsied. "My name is Alice." She motioned toward her companion. "And this is Peter—Peter Pan."

The little man said nothing in reply, but make no threatening move either. His eyes darted back and forth as if fearful that other strangers might be lying in wait.

"We're quite alone, I assure you," Alice said, sensing his concern. "And we didn't mean to upset you.

"You see, we're on our way to the Misty Mountains and we just happened upon your lovely hamlet. We won't be long and we'll try to be no bother to you."

After another uncomfortably long silence, the little man finally seemed to relax slightly.

"My name is Seela," he said in a high-pitched voice. "I am the head man of the village."

Pan coughed to keep from laughing at the very idea of this diminutive fellow being any sort of "man" at all! Alice glared at him and poked him lightly in the ribs with an elbow.

"You are welcome here," Seela said, lowering his staff.

(And how convenient, Alice thought, that he, like every other inhabitant of Neverland—including fairies, when they wanted to—she had thus far encountered, spoke the Queen's own *English*! The same had been true of those who dwelt in Wonderland, now that she thought about it. Most peculiar.)

The head man stepped forward, extending a short, stubby hand which first Pan and then Alice took gently and shook.

As if this was a prearranged signal, the doors of all the huts flew open and the rest of the inhabitants of the village spilled out. Pan and Alice quickly found themselves surrounded by smiling faces and chattering voices. None of the villagers was any taller than was Seela, with those who were actual children being smaller still. One woman held an infant that was no bigger than the toy doll Alice had played with as a little girl.

"We are called the *Diminii*," Seela said when at last the initial clamor had subsided.

"It's a pleasure to meet you all," Alice said. "Are there many of your people?"

"None, other than us, that I know of," Seela replied. "Are there many more like you?"

"Like me?" Alice wasn't sure what he meant.

"Yes." He motioned at her with an upward sweep of one hand. "So...*big!*"

Alice giggled. "I'm sorry. I don't mean to be impolite—but among *my* people, I wouldn't be considered to be very big at all. And yes, there are quite a lot of us."

"No offense," Seela said, "but I don't think I'd care to walk around with my head that far above the good earth."

"I'd never thought of it that way before," Alice said, "but you make a very good point."

"Is it possible we could spend the night here?" Pan interjected. "We've traveled quite a long ways, and it will be getting dark in just a few hours."

At the mere mention of nightfall, several gasps could be heard. A few of the Diminii actually scurried back into their huts and slammed the doors shut. Seela tried to ignore the slight uproar.

"Of course," he said, partially turning and waving a hand toward his own open doorway. "I hope you'll accept the hospitality of my own hut. It isn't much, but it's clean and warm."

"I'm sure that it will be wonderful," Alice said graciously, "and we're most grateful."

"We're glad to have you," Seela said, clearly warming to the two travelers. He stepped over to a pleasingly plump woman and gently ran the back of his callused hand across her rosy cheek; she smiled and inclined her head closer toward his.

"My wife, Animista," he said, and Alice again curtsied. (She was without a doubt the *most* curtsying girl he had ever met, Pan thought.)

"She's a wonderful wife," Seela said, causing the woman to blush. "A wonderful mother. And a wonderful cook."

"*Wonderful!*" Pan said enthusiastically.

"She's preparing a lovely vegetable stew for supper," Seela went on. "It will have potatoes and carrots and corn and squash—all grown right here."

"Sounds delicious," Pan replied, rubbing his hands together with relish. In gazing about as he had entered the village, he had noticed several pens holding small flocks of sheep as well as a few chickens walking about freely, pecking at the ground.

"And what sort of *meat* will we be having?" he asked.

At the very word, there came another loud, collective gasp of horror and several of the little people literally quaked.

"No meat!" Seela quickly (and far more loudly than should have been required for all to hear) declared. "We won't be eating any meat!"

"Oh?" a puzzled Pan said. "Why not?"

"Because meat is only for *us*," a deep and threatening voice said from behind the boy.

Pan and Alice slowly turned—and found themselves face-to-face with an enormous black *wolf*!

Chapter 17

Though his lips were curled back far enough to expose a row of deadly yellow fangs, the wolf made no move to attack. When he saw Pan's hand instinctively go to the hilt of his dagger, though, he growled and bristled— giving him the appearance of even greater size. (And he was already big enough for one of the little Diminii to have saddled and ridden like a horse!)

"No, Peter!" Alice pled, placing a restraining hand on the boy's arm.

"Look!" she whispered, pointing off to one side, where he saw three more wolves now come slinking out of one of the nearby fields to take up positions behind the black wolf.

The three new arrivals—a female and two half-grown male cubs—were dark gray in colour and not nearly so large as was the ebony head wolf of their pack family. But each was highly dangerous in its own right.

"Listen to your *mate*, hu-mon," the black wolf snarled. Flashes of silver tinged the tips of the wolf's dark fur; but they spoke not so much of age as of his ability to survive in the wild.

"Blackie" padded over to a spot where two stout, wooden stakes had been driven firmly into the ground. A short length of rope was secured around the top of each stake, hanging down to the ground.

"Where are tonight's offerings, Seela?" the wolf demanded of the leader of the Diminii.

"You've come sooner than was expected." The little man was trying to be brave, but faced by a murderous creature such as this he could not totally suppress the tremor in his voice.

"You and your family usually do not come until after full moonrise."

"But we're hungry *now*!" one of the cubs growled.

Blackie snapped at his impetuous son, sending him slinking away with his tail between his hind legs. "We can wait!" he commanded, then cast his baleful yellow eyes upon Seela.

"We'll be back at moonrise, hu-mon. You know what will happen if the offering is not here." The implied threat was plain.

"Yes," was all Seela could manage to say. He dabbed at his sweaty brow with a shaky hand as the small pack turned to make its way back into the forest.

"Wait!" Pan unexpectedly called out to the wolves. All eyes—human and animal—turned toward him in surprise.

"Can I come with you?" Pan asked to Alice's horror. A wily smile pulled up one corner of his mouth. "Just for a short visit, don't you know."

"And why would you want to do that, hu-mon?" the black wolf asked suspiciously. Pan flung his arms out to his sides.

"Because I think it would be an adventure!" he said glibly.

"Then, by all means, come along," Blackie said slyly. "And to make it an even bigger adventure—why don't you leave your weapons *here*?"

Pan laughed. "Why not? I wouldn't want you to be at a disadvantage—or to be *afraid*!"

Blackie growled low in his chest as Pan cavalierly handed his dagger and his pistol to a perplexed and worried Alice.

"You mustn't go with them, Peter!" Alice whispered with urgency. "They can't be trusted!"

"Fortunately," Pan said with a wink, "neither can *I*! And I've handled worse than old Blackie before, I'll have you know!"

"If you insist on doing this," she persisted, "at least let me go with you!"

"No."

"Why not?"

"Because, as you said, I can't trust them. That means I might not be coming back."

Alice was now even more worried. Though she'd known him but a short while, she'd never heard Pan contemplate aloud any possibility of failure or death.

"If there's any chance at all that you won't return—all the more reason not to go in the first place!"

He smiled rakishly. "But if you never take journeys from which you might not return—you'll never go anywhere at all! And where's the fun in that?"

As Alice and Pan conferred, the gray she-wolf moved up closer to her mate. "I don't trust this one," she hissed. "He's too *happy!*"

Blackie shrugged off her concerns. "Happy or unhappy—he's no threat to us." He then turned away and loped toward the outer edge of the village, his pack family behind and Pan bringing up the rear.

Pan turned only long enough to wave to Alice and Diminii. "I'll be back shortly," he bubbled. "Save me a bowl of stew!"

"Is your poor friend *insane?*" Seela asked Alice.

"Sometimes I think so," she said with a shrug. "But mostly I think he's just a boy."

Once back in the cover of the woods, the black wolf led his group back and forth in a confusing pattern that always turned to a deeper and thicker patch of forest.

"If he's trying to make sure I can never retrace my steps to his den," Pan thought, "he's wasting his time." He smiled at the very idea; the beast didn't know that the boy had a memory and a sense of direction that would have been the envy of any crow.

At last, though, they reached the low, vine-covered hillside that housed the den wherein the wolf pack dwelt. So thick was the foliage around it that one could easily have missed seeing the entrance at all.

The den was not very tall—there was no need for it to be to comfortably house four-legged creatures—nor terribly deep. Pan had to stoop slightly at the entrance in order to step inside.

The stench of the place slapped him so hard he nearly lost his last meal. The smell of wolf and wolf waste commingled with that of the bits of rotting flesh that still clung to some of the bones scattered about the floor of the den.

There was a constant buzzing to be heard and Pan found himself trying to wave away dark clouds of flies and gnats. He hoped not to be there long enough to become a haven for the fleas that doubtless also made their homes here.

"A fine house you have here!" he said to Blackie, rather proud of how easily the lie flew from his tongue. "And a fine family!" His eyes narrowed slightly then.

"But tell me something," he said. "I've always heard what fine *hunters* wolves are. Yet you seem to have given up hunting altogether."

"Why chase meat—when you can have it given to you?" Blackie replied.

"So you use your size and strength to terrorize those poor little people;

"SAVE ME A BOWL OF STEW."

you force them to do everything for you but chew the meat." Pan shook his head.

"You must be very *proud*," he added dryly.

"It's *meat* that fills empty bellies," the practical minded she-wolf declared. "Not *pride*."

"And after all," Blackie said, "we didn't *choose* to be wolves. That is simply who and what we are."

"Well, I daresay the people in that village didn't *choose* to be *slaves*, either," Pan countered.

"You make my point for me, hu-mon. That is simply who and what they are. We all have roles to play in life, and we play them."

"There's a difference you seem to be conveniently forgetting," Pan retorted, swatting at some winged nuisance that had alighted on his arm. "You may not have chosen to be a wolf—but nobody else *forced* you to be one."

Blackie chuckled, though his laughing sounded more like the wheezing of a steaming teakettle. "I suppose the little hu-mons decided it was better to be enslaved and alive—than free and *dead*!"

"And what do you suppose would happen if they decided this was *not* enough?" Pan posed. "What might happen if they decided to *resist* you instead?"

"That's easy to answer," Blackie replied with grim resolve. "We would then have to get used to hunting again…because they *and* their sheep would all be dead!"

Pan nodded but made no other reply for several tense moments. Then he smiled and clapped his hands together loudly, causing one of the cubs to jump and go into a defensive crouch.

"Well, I think my curiosity has been sufficiently satisfied," Pan said. "I must be on my way back to the village now; but I thank you for your warm hospitality!"

The cub he had startled leaped in front of him to bar his departure from the shallow cave, snarling and bristling in his best imitation of his sire. He was stunned when Blackie slammed into him with one hard shoulder, knocking him aside.

"You are free to go, hu-mon," Blackie growled.

"But take a warning with you. You and your mate must leave the place of the little hu-mons. Be far away from here by sundown tomorrow—or else!"

Pan nodded curtly in acknowledgment before stooping and making his exit from the fetid den.

Without the need to wind back and forth, he was able to head straight for the Diminii hamlet and reached it in good time. The first thing he saw was the head man Seela standing alone, leaning on his staff.

Pan came to stand beside him and saw that he was watching several of the village children at play. Alice was with them, clearly having taught them how to play the game "London Bridge." Pan smiled; it was good to see Alice for once freely engaging in decidedly non-adult entertainment.

"I'm glad to see you're alive," Seela said without taking his eyes off the cavorting youngsters.

"As always, I'm glad to *be* alive!" Pan replied. He, too, spent the next few minutes simply watching the children doing what all children everywhere should be able to do: enjoy themselves without a care in the world. At last, though, he drew in a deep breath and spoke again.

"As near as I could tell," he said, "there are only the four wolves—and two of them are only half grown."

"We already knew that," Seela replied stoically.

"You outnumber them," Pan declared. "You could fight them off."

"And how many of my people would *die* in the doing?" Seela said sadly. "No amount of sheep are worth a single Diminii life."

"And how much is *freedom* worth?" At these stinging words, Seela tore his eyes from the cheerful playing and looked at Pan.

"Do you have any children, sir?" he asked.

It felt incredibly strange to Pan to hear himself addressed as "sir." Then he remembered that he stood several inches taller than did the head man. To little Seela, Pan must have looked very grown up.

"No, I don't," he admitted.

"Then—and I mean no offense, sir—all *you* have to lose is your own life. We stand to lose much, much more."

Pan said nothing more for awhile; he just stood and watched the children at their play. He took note of how good Alice was with them and it pleased him to see this usually oh-so-serious girl now laughing and seeming to get fully into the spirit of fun for fun's sake.

"Your children really are beautiful, aren't they?" Pan observed.

"More lovely than the stars," Seela replied with heartfelt sincerity. "And more precious."

Pan grew silent again, swiveling his head to take in a view of some of the pens where the Diminii kept their animals.

"I have a question, friend Seela."

"Yes?"

"It's a simple question. Do you have *more* sheep now than you had *before* the wolves came?"

Seela took his time in answering, and his voice was low and filled with shame when at last he did.

"No."

"Do you have *fewer* sheep now?" Pan pressed relentlessly.

"Yes!" Now there was an angry edge to Seela's voice. "What is your *point*, sir?"

"I think you know the point, head man," Pan replied. He kept his eyes on the sheep in their pens, knowing that to look directly at Seela would only further shame the little man.

"Of *course* your flock is smaller. It takes far longer to birth and raise a lamb than it does to eat it. Which prompts a far more important question.

"Once the last sheep is gone…" Now he did turn to look Seela squarely in the eyes.

"What will the wolves eat *next*?"

Chapter 18

As the sun went down, head man Seela's wife Animista was lovingly tending to her large pot of simmering vegetable stew. She was being ably assisted in this chore by Alice, who had freely volunteered her services.

"Mmm," Alice moaned with delight, inhaling the smells rising up from the bubbling concoction. "It smells wonderful!"

"Wait until you taste it," Animista said. She withdrew the large wooden spoon with which she had been stirring the stew and offered Alice a taste. The girl blew a cooling breath on it, then sipped at it.

"Oh, my. It *is* delicious. There's much more flavor to it than I would have expected from just vegetables and water!"

"You can thank my husband for that," Animista said modestly. "He's the one who provides the herbs, roots and such that raise the flavor of the stew to a whole other level."

"Really?"

"Oh, yes. Seela grew up in the deep woods, you see. So he's an expert in finding such things—and at knowing which ones are edible and which ones are not safe to eat. Garlic, mushrooms, wild onions: you've seen what they do for a simple pot of stew."

She scooped up another spoonful of the stew and fed it to an appreciative Alice, who smacked her lips and licked them afterwards.

"He's usually in by now," Animista said, looking toward the door of their hut. "He knows supper will be on."

"Would you like me to go look for him?" Pan offered. He was stretched out on the earthen floor of the hut, playfully arm wrestling with both of Seela's young sons at the same time. He let them pin his arms down, then bounded to his feet.

There was no need, however, for at that moment the door opened inward and Seela strode through the portal. He leaned his staff against one corner of the hut, then removed a small rucksack carried on a strap over one shoulder and set it on the floor beside the crook.

Though he seemed a bit withdrawn and lost in thought, his wife smiled as he kissed her on the cheek and affectionately patted her ample bottom.

Even without meat, Pan and Alice found the meal politely presented to them to be also ample and quite filling and satisfying. In addition to the bowls of rich stew they were given thick slices of freshly baked bread sparsely smeared with a little tasty goat cheese.

Lifting his bowl up in both hands, Seela raised it to his lips like it was a tea cup and drained the last of his stew, then rose from his chair.

"It's time," he said grimly. "I need to be getting the sheep ready." As Animista had explained to Alice and Pan earlier, as head man of the village Seela had assigned to himself the distasteful job of selecting and staking out the sacrificial lambs for the wolves' consumption.

(The carnivorous beasts could, of course, have fairly easily leaped the fence that penned in the sheep and chased down their supper. But so complacent and lazy had they become that they demanded their offering be constrained and held in place for them. If not for the fact that they still favored the pleasure of the kill, they probably would have demanded that their wooly meals be served up to them on a platter!)

"Would you like me to come along and help?" Peter offered, starting to rise up from the table.

"Thank you, no, sir," Seela replied, laying a hand on Pan's shoulder and gently pushing him back down into his chair. "It wouldn't be right to ask a guest to participate in such dirty work."

Seela snatched his rucksack up off the floor, took hold of his staff and headed out the door.

"I wish he had accepted your help," Animista said just over half an hour later, wringing her hands. "He must be having some trouble getting a pair roped and tied up."

Pan glanced at Alice, who nodded. "Don't you worry," he said, rising up from his chair. "I'll go check on him; an extra pair of hands will help get the job done in no time."

He'd barely stepped away from his seat when the door of the hut swung inward, nearly hitting him. Seela entered, gave Pan a somewhat odd look, then turned away to put his gear up in the corner.

"It's done," was all he said. He then went and squatted before the fireplace, stretching his hands out and letting the flames leaping within it warm them. Animista walked over, bent and kissed him gently on the top of his head.

Within the hour…the otherworldly howling of the wolves began.

Their menacing yet mournful yowls filled the night air, seeming to come from all directions. As was always the case, the children were greatly frightened by the sound and crawled up onto their parents' laps in search of the comforting shelter of their arms. The adults stroked their hair and quietly assured them they were safe and had nothing to fear.

The nervous bleating of the lambs in the pens was the first sign that the wolves, having finished their serenade to the moon, were now loping on padded paws into the village proper.

Moments later, the sound of growling and fangs snapping blended with the terrified bawling of the two sacrificial sheep as the slaughter began. Alice reached out to grip Pan's hand and saw that his teeth were clenched as a mixture of anger and helplessness seized him.

Then, as quickly and as harshly as the sounds of struggle and death had begun—they ended. Silence filled the night.

Bang!

Something heavy slammed against the bolted door of Seela's hut, causing all inside to start in surprise and the children to cry out and burst into tears.

The banging noise was quickly followed by a softer but equally menacing sound. Claws could be heard scraping against the wood on the outside of the door. In response, Pan leaped to his feet and drew his dagger.

"No, Peter!" Alice implored, clutching at him. "Don't go out there!"

"No need to bother, sir," Seela said, holding up a cautionary hand.

The scratching stopped, only to be replaced by a nasty voice coming through the door. "I smell hu-mon," it said. "Maybe some night you'll tie one of your own to the stake!"

Pan cast questioning eyes at Seela, who only shook his head.

"It's just one of the cubs," he said wearily. "Sometimes they like to torment and taunt us by pretending they mean to break in. I think it gives them perverse pleasure, knowing how much it frightens the children."

"And not just the children," Animista said, hugging one of her own children more tightly to her bosom.

Pan made a growling sound of his own, born of indignation and frustration. He then sat down beside Alice, resigned to take no action.

The last, pitiable cries of the sacrificial sheep died away into wet gurgles. The wolves could be heard dragging the carcasses away, meaning to consume them back in their den. Nearly total silence draped the hamlet of the Diminii; the only sound was the muffled sobbing of some of the children huddled in their huts.

"We'd all best try to get some sleep," Seela said at last and began blowing out candles.

"Yes," Pan said. "And come morning…we'll take our leave." He was not so cruel as to add that he would be glad to have this place behind him.

Chapter 19

Breakfast the following morning consisted mainly of fried potatoes with a few precious eggs tossed in for extra flavoring. The meal was mostly eaten in silence.

The second he set his fork down on his empty plate, Pan rose to his feet. "Thank you," he said, directing his words at Animista. "But we'd best be going now."

"Do we need to be in such a hurry?" Alice asked, placing a hand on his arm.

"We've a long way to go," Pan replied. "And a clock that's not working in our favour."

"We understand," Seela said wearily (for he had gotten almost no sleep in the hours since the wolves had descended upon the hamlet), rising from his chair. "But before you go, sir—would you take a walk with me?"

Pan hesitated for a moment, then shrugged. "I suppose—so long as it doesn't take too long."

"It shouldn't." Seela retrieved his shepherd's staff from the corner and stepped through the door.

"Be ready to leave when I return," Pan told Alice before following the head man out of the hut.

He found Seela kneeling down beside the stakes where the two sacrificial sheep had been tied the night before. There was no sign of them now, save for streaks of blood left on the ground where their carcasses were dragged away by the wolves.

"You don't think very much of me, do you?" Seela said to Pan, not meeting his eyes.

"I like you and yours just fine, Seela," Pan replied. "And I guess I shouldn't expect everyone to face the world in the same way I do."

"Maybe we all have to find our own way," the little man said.

"Maybe so. I just hate to see good people treated so badly."

"That's because you're good, too. You're not a wolf." Seela returned to examining the tracks leading away from the stakes.

"Can you find your way back to their den?" he asked.

"Of course," Pan replied, puzzled. "But why would you want to go there?"

"I don't," Seela told him truthfully. "The very thought of it makes me want to run away. But there's something there I need to see."

"Very well," Pan said. "But you'd best keep that crook of yours ready, just in case."

With his own hand firmly on the hilt of his dagger, he set off at a brisk walk. It was difficult for Seela's shorter legs to keep up the pace but the Diminii did the best he could.

Pan slowed down as they drew near the hillock housing the wolves' den, moving more cautiously and quietly as he approached the entrance. His dagger was now out of its scabbard and thrust forward.

Which did him no good when, just as a stooped Pan entered the den, a large, furry object dropped straight down atop him!

It struck Pan in the chest, knocking him off his feet and landing squarely atop him. The boy cried out involuntarily, tensed in expectation of fangs and claws tearing into his flesh.

Amazingly, this did not happen; and he was able to push his way out from under the heavy mass of fur and regain his footing. Dagger raised to strike, he could clearly see now that it was one of the wolf cubs. Having dropped down on him off a narrow, rocky ledge, it now lay unmoving at Pan's feet.

And just as clearly...it was *dead*.

Pan knelt down to examine the body more closely. He jabbed it with the tip of his dagger's blade and found the corpse to be as stiff as wood.

The wolf's eyes were open but unseeing. Its fangs were exposed in one final, ferocious snarl. Flecks of white foam stained its lips and there were patches of coagulated blood under each nostril of its dark snout.

Just a step or two away, Pan and Seela nearly stumbled over the equally lifeless carcass of the first wolf's brother. Seela poked it sharply with the blunt end of his crook, assuring himself the creature was dead.

A low, painful moan then drifted to their ears, coming from the rear of the shallow cave. Alert, Pan and Seela pressed onward.

They found Blackie sprawled on his belly. Between moans, he panted heavily, his thick tongue lolling out of his gaping mouth. Like his sons, he had the white foam coating his lips and dark blood slowly oozed from his nostrils. Lying beside him was the body of his deceased mate.

"Dead," the black wolf groaned. "My entire family…they're all deeeaadd."

"And soon, you will be, too," Seela said. Pan was surprised by the coldness he heard in the little man's voice.

Blackie struggled to lift up his great, shaggy head. His eyes were starting to glaze over, but still he recognized the head man and fixed him with a baleful glare.

"*You!*" he snarled. "What did you do to us?"

Seela went down on one knee, staring intently at the wolf before answering his question.

"I've *killed* you," the little man declared, his tone surprisingly calm.

"But…but *how*, hu-mon?" The black wolf simply could not comprehend how such a thing could be possible.

"I *poisoned* you!" Seela said grimly, his childlike voice sounding defiant.

"What? How? *Uhnn!*" Blackie let out a moan and writhed on the floor of the den as sharp contractions twisted his belly.

"It was really quite easy," Seela said, confident that it was now he rather than the wolf that held the upper hand.

"I am expert at recognizing which plants are edible, which plants are beneficial, which plants have healing properties.

"And which plants can *kill!*"

Blackie writhed as if the words themselves were toxic.

"Last night," Seela went on, determined that the beast should know what had been his downfall, "I harvested plants I knew were poisonous and lethal—and I *fed* them to the two lambs I left out as sacrifice to you and your evil brood."

"No," Blackie groaned, his voice growing weaker.

"Yes. I fed them a blend of the toxic plants until I was sure their poor bodies were *full* of poison. And then *you* ate *them*.

"You were already as good as dead by the time the first pains would have twisted your innards." He leaned down even closer to the dying wolf.

"Now you know, you cursed wretch. Eventually…even *sheep* will strike back to save their own lives!"

"*I'll kill you!*" Blackie roared, lunging forward with his jaws opened wide to expose his flashing fangs. Startled, Seela fell over backwards.

This was literally Blackie's last gasp, though. He crashed to the ground mere inches away from sinking his teeth into Seela's leg and lay still.

Pan stepped close to the fallen wolf, prodding him sharply with the point of his dagger. When this elicited no response at all, he was satisfied that the great black wolf was truly dead.

Kneeling down beside the body, Pan used the sharp edge of his blade to saw off the wolf's large, fluffy tail. Rising, he held the grisly trophy out to Seela, who initially recoiled from its touch. Even when he did take it in his hand he seemed somewhat unresponsive as he strived to fully understand that the menace had indeed been completely eliminated.

"Tie this to the end of your staff," Pan directed. "That way, from now on, every man—and every beast—will know who you are.

"Seela—the Killer of Wolves!"

"Yes?" Seela mumbled numbly. "Well, right now, the killer's hands are shaking like a leaf in a gale!" The head man chuckled a bit, mostly in a bid to cover his very real trembling.

"Make no mistake," Pan said, growing serious. "What you did was very brave. And very risky. If they had survived your poisons—you'd have paid dearly."

"Yes; I'd thought of that many times. You see, I had considered trying this tactic before, almost every time I was in the woods gathering herbs and roots. But every time, I would fail to act on the thought. I was just too afraid.

"But your words and your example convinced me that I had to push back the fear and take action. I do not mind admitting to you that it was the hardest decision I ever made."

Pan put an arm around the Diminii's shoulders and led him from the den of death. "You certainly proved today that even a little body can house a very big heart!"

When the two of them emerged from the forest a short while later, they paused to look out over the village, which was coming to life in the morning sun. Unaware as yet of the fate of the wolf pack, the Diminii were dutifully going about their daily chores.

"Thank you for all you've done," Seela said to Pan. "You and your lady would be most welcome to stay on with us here forever."

"Thank you, friend Seela. That's a tempting offer; but we have to be on our way."

"I understand."

"I'll certainly try to return for a visit, though. And in the meantime, there *is* a small favor I would ask of you."

"Anything, sir."

"First off—you can stop calling me 'sir.' My name is Peter." Seela smiled and nodded.

"The other thing is more important. Tonight, I want you to host a big *celebration* for the entire village. Eat and drink. Sing and dance. Enjoy being alive."

"Gladly...Peter."

"And one more thing." Pan again threw an arm around Seela's shoulder and drew him closer.

"Make sure you add a little *mutton* to every pot of stew!"

Chapter 20

It was but a relatively short hike from the village of the Diminii to the next destination in their quest for treasure.

As she and Pan neared the base of the range of heights known as the Misty Mountains, Alice reflected upon the fact that she had now spent quite some time with this boy—alone. That is to say, without the company of a chaperone.

In proper circles, such a thing would be considered most *improper*. But Alice truly did not feel that she had done anything wrong or been guilty of any great impropriety. Time constraints and special circumstances surely mitigated her actions.

She was also fully aware of the fact that—aside from her occasional, brief contretemps with Peter, all this had done an admirable job of helping Alice not think over much about the passing of her parents and the circumstances awaiting her back home.

Home. Already it was beginning to feel as many years as it was miles away.

In general, the range of mountains they were approaching was neither terribly long nor terribly high. But in the very middle of it, side-by-side, were three peaks that did reach far into the sky.

"'Three there be'," Pan said, quoting the riddle and pointing to the trio of heights.

"But which one?" Alice asked. "Surely we don't have time to climb all three."

"The one in the middle," Pan replied.

"How can you be sure?"

"Look at it Alice. It's the tallest of them all. So high you can't see the top of it for the clouds." He turned his eyes to her but saw only a puzzled expression.

"'The hole in the clouds'," he said, again quoting the riddle.

"And it *does* seem like it could reach to the stars," Alice reflected. "How ever will we find a single little chest in such an immense place?"

"By climbing it, I suppose," Pan said. "So we'd best get to it."

And climb they did. And with each foot higher they rose, so did it seem the temperature fell. By the time they reached the lower portions of the perpetual cloud bank obscuring the top of the peak and stopped to take a rest, both were hugging themselves and stomping their feet in an effort to stay warm.

"I wonder about poor Tink," Alice ruminated. "While the two of us are traipsing all about Neverland...is she even still alive? Are those monsters treating her humanely?"

Pan gave a short, humorless laugh. "Are we facing enough *responsibility* to suit you, Miss Grown-Up?" he said sarcastically.

"And are you facing it better than a *child* would, Mister Never-Grow-Up?" Alice retorted, sticking her tongue out at him.

Pan's only response was a scowl, but her remark had disturbed him far more than Alice realized. She didn't understand just how the very idea of growing up horrified him.

"We'd best keep moving," was all he said.

Climbing through the layer of clouds was worse than making one's way through one of the famous London fogs. They could barely see well enough to find suitable purchase for their hands and feet. Their own breath came out as small clouds that left tiny crystals of ice in their hair.

And they were momentarily blinded when at last they suddenly broke through the blanket of clouds—for here the sunshine was bright and reflecting even more brightly off patches of snow everywhere.

They stood silent for a time, letting their eyes adjust and gazing at the barren vastness around and above them.

"It's beautiful, in its own way," Alice gasped, gazing at the awe-inspiring tableau. "But there's still so *much* of it. Wherever might a chest be hidden in it?"

"Given how difficult it's been to find the others," Pan said, applying a certain sort of logic as he pointed upward, "it's probably at the very top!"

"Probably so," Alice glumly admitted.

From somewhere in the barren wilds looming above them, a sound now drifted down to them. Sounding a bit like a mix of a lion's roar and a bull elk's trumpet, it was enough to make already frigid blood run even colder.

"What kind of beast was *that*, Peter?" Alice asked.

"None I've ever heard before," he told her. "And from the sound of it—none I ever care to meet!"

Still, they felt they had no choice but to continue their climb. Luckily, Pan's keen eyes detected a sort of narrow pathway that made their passage through the outcroppings of rock easier.

So intently were the children's eyes fixed on that path, though, that neither of them saw or heard the shaggy, shadowy figure that was now stalking them from above.

At one point in the assent the pathway widened a bit, so they decided to again pause to catch their breaths.

"I *do* so wish we had time to build a fire," Alice moaned. "It's starting to feel like I'll never be warm again!"

"I'm not sure we could start one even if we did have the time," Pan said, his teeth chattering slightly as he peered about them.

"This high up, there aren't many trees to supply firewood."

"But a girl can dream," Alice said, and they both chuckled softly.

But the laughter died in their throats when the great, hairy beast then dropped down between them!

Chapter 21

Alice had never seen such a creature before; she had never even *read* of such a creature!

It stood at least eight feet tall and was covered from head to toe by a thick coat of matted, dirty white fur. Its face looked slightly like that of a man but more like that of a great ape. It stood upright like a man, on enormous, furry feet. Claws tipped each finger of its hands and the roar that issued from it would freeze lava in its tracks.

Staggering as she tried to back away from the monster, Alice caught her heel on a rock and toppled over backwards onto the snowy ground. Seeing its prey vulnerable, the snow monster stalked toward her.

Pan, recovering his own balance in the wake of the beast's initial attack, now took to the air. Like an annoying mosquito, he began to buzz around the head of the monster.

As Alice regained her footing, she saw the creature swatting at Pan with its massive hands. Knowing that one swipe of its claws could spell the end for Peter, she frantically looked about for any object that might serve her as a weapon.

All that came to hand was a rock, approximately the size of an apple. Alice would have done any cricket pitcher proud as she reared back and flung the stone. Still, it was sheer chance that guided the rock on a path that led it to strike directly on the end of the monster's nose.

"*Ow!*" it yelped loudly.

As the beast stopped and slapped both hands over its injured nose, Peter saw his chance and drew out his dagger.

"Stop!" Alice shouted up to him. With another rock now in hand, she cautiously approached the monster. Instead of a roar, it was now more of a gravelly whine that escaped its lips.

"Did you just say 'ow'?" Alice asked him.

"Of *course* I did!" the monster replied, its voice somewhat muffled by the furry hands covering his face.

"What would *you* say if you'd just been bopped on the snout with a rock?"

"Well, the truth is—I didn't expect you to say anything at all," Alice said.

As Alice spoke, she stepped closer to the groaning creature and let the rock drop out of her hand. Pan, still hovering in the air, did not think this to be a well-advised move on Alice's part, given that she was approaching a beast that could probably swallow her nearly whole. But he said nothing, fascinated by what was unfolding below him.

"After all," Alice continued, speaking in slow, measured tones, "you *are* just an animal—aren't you?"

"Just listen to *you*," the beast snarled. "As if being 'just an animal' isn't good enough!"

"But you *did* plan to kill and eat us, didn't you?" Pan accused while still remaining beyond the creature's reach.

"Well...*yes*," the monster conceded. He removed his hands from his face, then gingerly touched the tip of his nose with one finger. It was beginning to swell, but did not appear to be broken. He then spread his apish arms out in both directions.

"But just look around you. What *else* is there to eat?" He wrapped his great arms around himself and shivered.

"Not that you two little tidbits would be enough to keep me comfortable in this infernal *cold!*"

"Doesn't your *fur* keep you warm?" Alice asked. Strangely, though she was now facing a frightful beast, she felt in little more danger than she would have in her own parlor.

"It keeps me from *freezing*," the creature growled, "but that's not the same as being warm!"

Pan gave him a quizzical look. "Well, if you're so miserable here, they why don't you just go somewhere else—where it's warmer and there's more food?"

"Where else *is* there?" the not-so-abominable snowman asked earnestly.

He pointed up. "Where the world ends up there is just as barren."

He pointed down toward the cloud cover. "And where the world ends down there is just as cold!"

"Oh, my goodness," Alice said, gazing down at the cloud deck through which she and Pan had passed earlier. "That isn't the end of the world."

"It isn't?"

"Of course not," Pan said with exasperation. "Where do you think *we* came from?"

"I really hadn't given it any thought," the snowman confessed, "beyond what a fine meal the two of you would make!"

"You're not very smart, are you?" Pan said.

"As smart as one needs to be in a place like this," the beast replied in his own defense.

"I'm just not very *curious*," he said. "This is the only world I've ever known—so I thought it was the only world at *all*!"

"There's a great, big, beautiful world down below the clouds," Alice told him. "Maybe more than one."

"Is it warmer than this one?" the snowman asked hopefully.

"Some places are downright *hot*," she said. "If you'd like, we could accompany you down below the clouds so you can see for yourself."

"You'd do that for me?" the snowman asked, not sure he had heard her correctly (what with his ears being covered by the shaggy hair on his head and all). "Even though I intended to have you for my supper?"

"You just didn't know any better, that's all," Alice said brightly.

"Then, yes—I'd very much like you to show me the way!"

"Well, if we're going to be traveling together," Alice said, "we should first introduce ourselves. My name is Alice."

"And you may call me *Yeti*," the snowman said.

"Yeti it is, then."

"Ahem," Pan coughed.

"Oh," said Alice. "And this is my friend, Mister Peter Pan."

"*Ahem!*" Peter coughed even louder. He was "standing" in midair, arms folded across his chest, one foot impatiently tapping at empty space.

"Haven't you forgotten something, Alice?"

"No; I don't think so."

"Not even our reason for *being* here?"

"Oh, no!" Alice cried, blushing deeply. "Before we can leave here, we have to find the *riddle* we're looking for. Can *you* help us find it, Mister Yeti?"

"I will if I can," the snowman said. Then his brow furrowed in thought. "Can you tell me what a riddle looks like?"

"A riddle is simply words written on a piece of paper," Alice patiently explained, while Pan slapped his head in great *imp*atience.

"Every one we've found so far has been inside a small box, like so," Alice said, using her hands to show roughly the dimensions of the previous riddle chests they had seen.

"Why, I think I know *exactly* where such a thing is!" Yeti declared. "Follow me."

The two children did as he asked. Yeti's big, hairy feet did an excellent job of stamping down the snow as he walked, making the way much easier for Pan and Alice. Still, Alice couldn't help but notice that Peter's right hand never strayed far from the hilt of his dagger.

"I think it's a lucky thing we stumbled upon this poor creature," Alice whispered.

"Let's make sure he's not leading us to his *kitchen* before we decide how lucky we are!" Pan replied.

Yeti led them slightly higher up the mountain before coming to the mouth of a cave, which he entered without hesitation. Even Alice was a bit leery of following him here; but as there was really little other choice, she shrugged and stepped boldly forward.

The air was still cold inside the cavern, but felt a bit warmer by comparison since it at least provided shelter from the frigid winds that swirled around the mountain continuously.

"This is where I live," Yeti announced.

The cave was decidedly lacking in the comforts of home. There were no furnishings to speak of. In one corner sat a small pile of *bones*: all that remained of some of Yeti's previous meals. And the musky odor associated with an animal's warren caused Alice's nose to crinkle. Still...

"It's very nice," she said, feeling one should be polite even to an abominable snowman. Pan gawked at her as if she had lost her mind.

"I think the thing you want is up here," Yeti said, pointing to an outcropping of rock several feet above the cave floor. He then put his massive hands around Alice's waist and lifted her off her feet!

"Oh!" she gasped and Pan took a step forward, starting to draw his dagger.

" CAN YOU TELL ME WHAT A RIDDLE IS? "

But Yeti had no malicious intent in his action; he was merely lifting Alice up so she could reach the small chest and get it herself.

Once she had done so, he immediately set her back down, with surprising gentleness. She handed the chest to Pan, who studied it intently. He would see what were clearly the marks left by fangs and claws on its lacquered surface.

"Did you try to open this?" he asked Yeti.

"Oh, no," the snowman replied. "I tried to *eat* it. When I realized it wasn't food," he gave a hairy shrug, "I lost interest in it and tossed it up there."

He gazed longingly out the mouth of his cave. "Can we go to the place that's less cold now?" he asked.

"Gladly," Pan replied.

"If you'll allow me," Yeti growled, "I think I can make the journey a quicker one for you."

"That would be lovely," Alice replied, then exclaimed, "Oh!" as Yeti plucked both her and Pan off the ground and deposited them atop his broad, furry shoulders.

With Yeti as their conveyance, they did indeed make the trip back down the mountain in much less time than it had taken them to ascend it.

Upon reaching the foot of the Misty Mountains, Yeti set them back on the ground, then stood gazing around him in near stupefaction. Everything he looked upon was new to him: the grass between his hairy toes, the verdant trees, the sound of birds on the wing.

And for the first time in his life, however long that had been, he did not feel *cold*. This new found sensation of warmth alone was enough to melt his shaggy heart.

"Thank you," he said to Alice, his voice breaking as he took both her hands in one of his. "You've brought me to a whole new world, a whole new life."

"You're most welcome, Mister Yeti," Alice replied, rewarding him with a smile that left him feeling an entirely different sort of warmth.

"Let this be a lesson," she said in a kind voice. "One should never think that all he *sees* of the world is all there *is* of the world."

"I'll try to remember that," Yeti replied.

"Peter and I will be moving on from here shortly," Alice told the snowman, "as we're on a most important mission. Would you like to come with us?" Pan scowled at this, but said nothing.

Yeti pondered the invitation for quite some time (having never before needed to give much thought to anything other than what to eat and when to sleep) before he responded.

"I think I'd rather go off alone," he said. "It's what I'm used to being and I would like to take my time in exploring this big, new world you've introduced me to." He smiled at Alice, then frowned.

"If that's all right?" he added, not wishing to offend or seem ungrateful.

"It's quite all right," Pan said quickly. He patted the hairy snowman on one arm. "Don't let us keep you."

It occurred to Alice that Cheshire Cat had responded in virtually the same way earlier. She rather envied him and Yeti. She too was exploring Neverland—but not at all in the relaxed way she would have preferred.

"Good-bye, Mister Yeti," she said. "Do be careful."

"You, too. Good-bye!" And with that, Yeti took his leave of them, crashing through the underbrush in pursuit of a colorful butterfly that had caught his eye.

"Be careful, Mister Yeti," Peter mocked, using the gift he had for mimicry to sound just like Alice. "Huh! It's the *rest* of the world that will have to be careful of *him*!"

"Don't be silly," Alice rebuffed. "He's just an innocent."

"Indeed. An innocent that could kill and devour a *cow* in less time than it would take you to prepare tea!"

Alice shrugged. "Well, as he said—he's got to eat *something*!"

Pan shook his head, then glanced up at the sky. "It'll be dark soon. We might as well make camp for the night and get a fresh start in the morning."

Alice was still chilled from her stay in the mountains, so the prospect of a warm fire was most agreeable to her. Along with a meal of their simple but filling stores, it left her feeling much improved.

"I suppose we should read the riddle now," she said finally. Pan handed the most recently acquired chest to her.

"Be my guest."

As anticipated, Alice found yet another parchment scroll rolled up inside the box. Unfurling it, she read the riddle aloud.

Only that which is alive can grow,
A simple truth we all do know.
But the rope of time brings pain and strife,
And the living thing can take a life.

Pan leaned over, covering his face with his hands. "Why can't these bloody riddles ever lead us to a *happy* place?" he moaned.

"Why?" asked Alice. "Where will this one take us?"

"A place fit only for death," Pan replied, staring grimly at her. "*The Hangman's Tree!*"

Chapter 22

The sound of brittle human bones crunching beneath the weight of her slippered feet sent waves of revulsion racing up and down Alice's spine.

"These be the bones of pirates," Pan said ominously.

"But why are they littered around on the ground instead of being decently buried beneath it?" Alice asked.

"This is what I've heard," Pan explained. "When a pirate dies at sea—whether of natural causes or by virtue of being shot, stabbed, walking the plank, being left on Marooner's Island, or strung up from the yardarm—his body is immediately consigned to the depth of the sea.

"If he commits a crime on dry land, though, he is brought here—where he is hanged by the neck until he is dead.

"There's no buryin' done, then. Instead, he's left dangling as a warning to any others who might be tempted to break the pirate's code. Time and predators eventually consume his flesh and his bones are all that remain, littering the ground all round the tree."

"But—so *many*?" Alice asked.

"That's because every execution carried out, for as long as most folk can remember, was done right here—at the Hangman's Tree."

"But why here? What makes this place so special?"

"Because the buccaneers consider this spot to hold the perfect tree for carrying out that kind of awful business.

"Look at it," Pan said, pointing to the tree they stood under.

"It has a stout branch that protrudes at just the right angle, exactly parallel to the ground. And it's just the right height above the ground and just the right width to bear the weight of even the heaviest of condemned prisoners."

While Pan spoke almost admiringly of this terrible instrument of execution, Alice was horrified by it. She noted that while there were plenty of other, perfectly normal trees hereabout, none of them grew within a hundred feet of this one. It stood alone in this bone-strewn clearing; it was as if all the other trees shunned it because of the grisly use to which it was put.

The Hangman's Tree looked incredibly old and gnarled. Its lower limbs were bare, devoid of all foliage, but clusters of leaves did sprout outward and upward from its upper branches.

In silent agreement, Alice and Pan separated and began to walk in slow circles all around the tree, searching for a chest hidden amidst the layers of dry bones.

Finding nothing, Alice begrudgingly approached the base of the tree. The rope and noose used to carry out the hangings was dangling from its lowest branch. It was, she thanked the stars, empty at the moment. Still, the fact that it was swaying ominously back and forth even though there was not the slightest breeze filled the girl with dread.

It occurred to her that the next riddle chest in their quest might be hidden from view within the leafy branches at the top of the tree; she doubted that any of the piratical executioners had ever bothered to look any higher than the branch from which they hanged their helpless victims.

Seeing that Pan was still exploring the bony debris away from the tree, and saying not a word to him, Alice jumped up, grabbed a branch and pulled herself up into the tree.

Like such childish things as playing with dolls, leaping into piles of autumn leaves and laughing for the sheer joy of it, Alice had long since left her tree climbing days behind her. Yet she found that the required skills came back to her fairly quickly and she made good time weaving her way upward.

Until, that is, when she was more than halfway up the tree's height—something grabbed hold of the hem of her dress.

Assuming she had simply snagged the cloth on the end of a bare branch, she looked down.

And found herself gazing straight down into a pair of large, hate-filled *eyes*—that were set right in the trunk of the tree!

Chapter 23

Below those baleful eyes, a large, gaping *mouth* next appeared in the bole of the Hangman's Tree.

Clearly, this horrendous tree was alive. Not alive in the way all trees and shrubbery and other kinds of greenery are; oh, no.

Alive in the way a wild animal might be!

Nor had Alice's dress merely caught on one of its random branches. An entire limb was now moving about much like a human arm. The gnarly "hand" at the end of that branch had grabbed hold of the dress, which now suffered a rip several inches long.

Alice screamed—instantly alerting Pan. Realizing in a heartbeat what was happening, he took flight toward the tree, intent on rescuing Alice from its clutches.

Even as he did so, the tree limb that had torn Alice's dress then grabbed her around the waist.

Pan now found that reaching the girl was going to be no easy task. Several of the tree's limbs began to flail about, swatting at him. Alice couldn't help but think that the tree reminded her of a very old statue she had once seen in a museum, depicting some ancient deity that had multiple arms.

Pan was as quick and nimble as he was fearless and he dodged back and forth to avoid the flailing tree branches. There were so many of them, though, that one eventually connected solidly with his jaw, sending him plummeting to earth.

With the wind thoroughly knocked out of him, Pan struggled to catch his breath. As he attempted to push himself up off the ground, he heard Alice scream again.

Even as the cursed tree continued to hold Alice in its grasp, the limb from which the hangman's noose dangled bent and moved up toward her—until the noose went over her head and settled around her neck.

Clearly—the tree intended to *hang* poor Alice!

Shaking the cobwebs out of his rattled skull, Pan leaped to his feet; but this time he did not fly blindly forth to physically confront the animated tree.

Queen Sangramore had called him clever—so he needed to *be* clever!

Alice struggled in vain to wriggle her way free of the wooden hand that held her. Failing that, she reached up to pull the noose loose from round her throat. Her efforts were foiled, though, when yet another branch snaked out and pinned her arms to her sides. It looked hopeless.

"Hey! Look at me, you decrepit pile of rotten mulch!" a voice called from the base of the tree.

Both the tree and Alice looked down to see that Pan was now standing at the foot of Hangman's Tree, a cocky smile on his face.

"You'd best release my friend, you aging rest home for toothless termites!"

"Or else *what*?" Alice called down without thinking; then clamped her mouth shut.

"Or else *this*!" Pan shouted. He raised both hands—in which he held his strike-a-light. He tapped flint and steel together, sending sparks flying toward the bole of the tree.

There are very few things that frighten a full-grown tree: high winds, lightning. But, as Pan well knew, the very thing they all feared the most— was *fire*!

For the first time, an actual sound came from the mouth of the Hangman's Tree. It was a loud but pitiful shriek. In a panic, it began trying to swat at Peter with all its arms; but the boy was so close to its trunk that they could not reach him.

Bringing all its animated limbs to the task of swatting at Pan necessitated pulling the noose off Alice and releasing its hold around her body. With more than a few bangs and bumps along the way, Alice fell out of the tree, landing with a loud thump on the ground beside Peter.

Her ungracious descent had also resulted in a few of the tree's shorter, dryer branches snapping off and these too fell at Pan's feet.

"Hold one of them up for me!" he called to Alice, and she quickly did so. He expertly used his strike-a-light to ignite one end of it, creating a torch to use as a weapon.

Pan started the wave it back and forth and the frightened tree began to scream louder and try to twist away from the dreaded flame (much as the cave-dwelling serpents near the Mermaids' Lagoon had done earlier).

The tree jerked back and forth violently until it appeared its trunk was cracking in half. This was in fact its way of developing a pair of "legs" beneath its branches.

As though mired in quicksand, it tried desperately to pull itself up and out of the ground from which it grew.

"*Yi-yi-yi!*" Pan shouted, continuing to threaten the tree by waving his torch to and fro before its crazed eyes.

Screaming eerily from its efforts, the tree finally succeeded in pulling free from the soil. As it did, its "feet" were revealed to be two large and tangled clumps of *roots*—which both nourished it and kept it locked in place.

Slightly dazed from her fall, Alice now found herself having to duck beneath the rising roots and dodge large clumps of hardened dirt that were flung from them.

As she did so, however, Alice was also able to catch sight of a small object that had been buried alongside the tree and had long since become entangled in the web of its root system.

The object was a small *chest*—virtually identical to the three others that had held the riddles she and Pan sought!

Forgoing any thoughts for her own safety, Alice dived right into the midst of the root network that held the chest in its clutches. Even as she began to twist and claw her way through the tangle, the tree raised one of its legs and tried to shake her off.

It felt to Alice almost as if she was again aboard her storm-tossed raft near Skull Rock, but she dug in even harder. She blinked and spit as sprays of dirt swirled around her.

"Yes!" she cried out when her efforts paid off and her fingers fell upon the chest.

She pushed and she pulled; she pulled and she pushed. She clawed with her hands like a dog after a bone.

The tree's leg jerked spasmodically and this time Alice was flung away from it. She bounced once, twice and even a third time; the dry bones that were her only cushion clacked as they shattered beneath her.

As quickly as could possibly be expected, she was back on her feet and prepared to dive again into the tangle of roots. Then her eyes fell upon the small chest lying nearby; she had managed to pull it free and hang onto it even as she was being ejected from the tree.

"I've got it, Peter!" she shouted happily, holding the chest over her heart in both hands. "I've got the chest!"

But for the moment, Pan ignored her; if he even heard her at all. He was continuing to threaten Hangman's Tree with fire.

Desperate to escape its nemesis, the tree turned and fled. Its steps were decidedly slow and awkward, looking somewhat like the gait of a circus performer on stilts. (In the tree's defense, allowances have to be made. This was, after all, the very first time it had attempted to walk!) Its strides were long as well as clumsy, and would soon carry it out of sight.

Pan made no real effort to pursue it, though he continued to yell insults at it and wave his torch in a threatening fashion. The animated tree's screams of terror also continued and could be heard even after it had fled from sight.

The flames at the end of the torch having nearly gone out, Pan puffed hard enough to completely extinguish what remained. Tossing the scorched branch aside, he turned to see Alice seated on the ground, holding the newest chest in her lap.

As he walked toward her, though, he changed his gait to imitate the awkward stride of the Hangman's Tree. He waved his arms like branches and made a howling noise that sounded exactly like that wooden monster.

"I'm coming for you, little girl!" Pan growled as he drew close to Alice.

Much as she hated to encourage his silliness, Alice couldn't stop herself from smiling, then giggling, and then laughing out loud. Pan flopped down beside her and joined in the laughter.

Neither of them noticed a large *owl* that had come to perch on the limb of one of the ordinary trees that grew around the edges of the bone-filled clearing.

Nor did they see the bird's large, peering eyes begin to glow redly.

Alice *did* note that Peter's laughter had taken on a rather choked sound before it stopped altogether.

Then the boy's eyes seemed to roll to the top of their sockets just before he pitched over in a faint!

Chapter 24

omewhere out at sea, the pirate's brig called the *Jolly Roger* rode high in the water.

Inside the cabin of its captain, suspended from a ceiling beam, dangled the tiny birdcage that held the fairy Tinker Bell as its tiny prisoner.

Inside the cage, the forlorn Tink picked listlessly at a small biscuit; this and a thimble of water had served as her only daily rations since she had been taken captive.

The cabin door opened and in strode Captain Hook himself, arrogantly puffing on his twin cigars.

"How's our little lady doing today?" he said with faked solicitude.

He showed his true nature by blowing an acrid puff of smoke into the birdcage, stinging Tink's eyes and inflaming her little lungs. He then harshly slapped the cage, causing it to spin round and round. By the time it stopped, poor Tink was totally disoriented and lying upside down, pressed against one side of the cage with her feet up in the air.

"You're a mean man, James Hook," Tink scolded once she had regained her equilibrium and was again upright on both feet.

"Yes," he surprisingly agreed.

"You're cruel."

"Yes," he said even more emphatically.

"You're...you're..." Tink struggled to find the right word.

"You're *evil*!" she hissed.

"*Yes*!" Hook practically screamed. "Of *course* I am!"

He began to laugh that terrible laugh that only truly wicked people seem capable of producing, while he danced a sort of jig from one foot to the other. He then thrust his face up close to the bars of the birdcage.

"We're *all* evil, little lady," he sneered, "to one extent or another. Even *fairies*!"

Tink shrank back from him in shame. It was almost as if his piercing eyes had looked right into her soul and witnessed some of her past deeds that could certainly not be characterized as being good.

"All the do-gooders strive to teach us that we must fight against our evil impulses," Hook continued.

"But that sort of struggle is extremely tiring. It requires so much time and energy—especially given that it so seldom seems to yield any good result.

"Why, being good might even be...*unnatural!*" He made a loud tsking sound with his tongue against the back of his teeth.

"Why not save all that wasted time and energy—and just give in to the more natural impulse to be evil?" The pirated grinned wickedly.

"It's actually quite *fun* to be evil—once you get the hang of it!"

He then smiled *extra* wickedly and pressed his face even more fully against the bars of the birdcage.

"Who knows," he said in an oily tone that almost dripped venom. "After supper tonight—I may give in to temptation and *pluck* them shiny, silly little wings right off your shoulders!"

Hook fully expected this threat to elicit a reaction of anguish, fear and horror from Tinker Bell.

What he got instead—was a punch on the tip of his pirate nose by a tiny fairy fist!

"*Yoww!*" he yelled, more in surprise and anger than from actual pain, then gave the cage another furious spin.

Moaning and muttering invectives to himself, the pirate captain staggered to a back corner of his cabin and threw himself down upon a cushioned seat in front of a large, expensive harpsichord.

The musical instrument was one of his few possessions that he had purchased rather than stolen. He ran his long fingers across the keys from one end to the other before settling down to playing an actual tune.

Even in her dizzy condition, Tinker Bell could tell it was a lovely melody and that Hook played it masterfully. (Even an evil person can be possessed of talent—though more often than not they find a way to corrupt it or turn it to some foul use.)

Tink would never have told Hook so, but he was a handsome man in a dangerous sort of way (for evil things are often hidden in pretty packages). That beauty could quickly turn ugly, as she had just witnessed; his eyes had even taken on a red glow when she had struck him.

She shook her tiny head. How, she wondered, was it at all possible that something so wondrous as this music (played by a man with only five fingers and a hook, remember!) could come pouring out of so black a heart?

The moment was broken by the door of the cabin being flung open so strongly that it banged against the wall. Through the opened portal breezed the haughty Queen Sangramore—accompanied as always by her devoted crocodile.

Hook's performance on the harpsichord ended abruptly with a cacophonous clang as he banged his hands down on its keys whilst he leaped to his feet and backed into a corner.

Chapter 25

"Why do you always have to bring that vile creature along with you?" Hook demanded, pointing at the crocodile.

"I suspect if he could talk he would ask me the same question about *you*, dear boy," the Queen of Diamonds said airily. At this the crocodile licked his lips in a most disconcerting and disgusting manner, spraying droplets of saliva across the floor of the cabin.

"Besides, it isn't so much that I bring him anywhere," the Queen asserted. "He simply likes to follow me around!"

She bent down and the beast raised its great head to allow her to scratch under his leathery chin.

"And who could say no to that face? Who's a good boy?" Sangramore cooed in the way one would talk to a baby. "Who's Mommy's good boy?"

The crocodile seemed almost to smile and again made that reptilian equivalent of a purring sound that so appalled Captain Hook.

"But enough of this," Sangramore said sharply, turning her eyes toward the pirate.

"I've just received word from the owl familiar I sent to spy on Peter Pan and the girl. It seems I chose my agents wisely. He and that sickeningly sweet girl have seemingly succeeded every step of the way thus far; and I have every reason to believe they will continue to do so."

"Peter I understand," Tinker Bell said. Her equilibrium had not yet fully returned, so she clung tightly to the thin but sturdy bars of her cage.

"But why the girl? Why did you drag Alice into your horrid scheme?"

"Should I tell her?" Sangramore spoke not to Tink but to the crocodile. "Should Mommy tell the little bug?"

"*Hey!*" Tink exclaimed angrily.

The crocodile gave forth a low, rumbling, menacing growl.

"Very well," the queen chirped. "I'll tell her. After all, who doesn't enjoy a good story?" She stepped close to the birdcage that held Tink captive, peering inside.

"And if you behave yourself until I've finished—I *might* see fit to feed you something a little better than biscuits!"

With little choice in the matter, Tink turned her empty water thimble upside down and took a seat on it. With one hand, she silently motioned for the Queen of Diamonds to proceed with her story.

"Finding sweet Alice was pure happenstance," Sangramore began. "You see, while all the other inhabitants of Wonderland were utterly content to waste their time and their lives having tea parties, playing croquet and generally being crazy—*I* aspired to loftier heights.

"It took me quite a while—I did have to take time now and again to prevent my dear, addled sister the Queen of Hearts from lopping off heads wholesale—and quite a lot of study and work—two pursuits practically unheard of in Wonderland.

"But at long last, I discovered the means to leave Wonderland whenever I liked, and to travel elsewhere.

"Now, I'll admit to being mildly perturbed to find that I could only travel to two other places; but even that was blessed relief. After all, even the sanest person, if forced to live constantly in a madhouse, will eventually become mad, too. I barely escaped that fate."

Tink opened her mouth to voice the opinion that Sangramore had not left Wonderland nearly soon enough, then closed it. Listening to this rambling discourse was still less boring than simply staring out the bars of her cage.

Plus, she really *would* like a taste of something other than biscuits.

The queen had paused, sensing the fairy was about to interrupt her fascinating narrative. When Tink didn't, though, Sangramore continued.

"As I was saying. There were only two other places I could go: here to Neverland and to that dreary spot Alice and her kind so arrogantly like to think of as the *Real* world.

"It didn't take long, once I was here, before I began to hear stories about a wondrous boy called Peter Pan and of his many bold adventures—especially his feud with the pirate Captain Hook.

"Of the two, I found Hook to be the more fascinating." She paused to look toward Hook, pursing her lips as if throwing a kiss in his direction. He grinned like an infatuated schoolboy.

"The stories, of course," Sangramore went on, "told of Hook's unfortunate demise at the hand of Pan and in the belly of the crocodile." She blew the beast a kiss now and Hook scowled jealously.

"But the gossip was that the crocodile had for no apparent reason taken up permanent residence in a small and isolated inlet, from which it seemed never to stray far."

Captain Hook did not really need to hear the queen's narration from this point, for he had been an active participant in the events that followed.

He didn't know how long he had been a prisoner inside that damp and smelly cave; the days and nights had all begun to blend hopelessly together. Alone, bereft of hope, he teetered on the brink of madness. He had even begun to think of ending it all by simply throwing himself into the lagoon and letting the crocodile feast upon him!

He thought his mind had completely left him the day he looked up from his dark thoughts and saw a vision of loveliness gliding into his stony prison.

With the crocodile docilely walking beside her. (How she ever managed to get the lumbering beast up the rocks and into the cave, Hook never bothered to ask.)

In no time, Hook had sworn to Sangramore on bended knee that if she would only free him from his captivity and protect him from the crocodile he would faithfully serve her.

The Queen of Diamonds accepted his offer and his terms.

"It seems to me the first thing we must do," she told him, "is deal with this problem between you and my precious new pet."

She knelt down beside the beast and used the strange ability she had roughly to communicate with him.

"He's trying to tell me something about—a clock?" she said, somewhat puzzled. Hook quickly explained the situation to her.

"Then the answer seems obvious," Sangramore declared. "If we can cure the poor baby's...digestive ills...he will be much more useful to me.

"And if we can restore his ability to experience the full taste of other foods—perhaps his inordinate appetite for pirate parts might at least diminish if not disappear entirely."

"And how do you propose we go about doing that, m'lady?" Hook asked, not daring to hope.

"Watch and learn," was all she said, then began lightly to stroke the side of the crocodile.

In a very short time, the toothy amphibian had been lulled into a stuporous, somnambulant state of near unconsciousness. Hook again wondered if he was hallucinating when he saw Sangramore grab hold of the crocodile's upper snout and open his mouth wide with her bare hands!

"Get down here, Captain," she instructed, jerking her head. "Stick your arm down his gullet and pull out that bloody clock!"

"Are you *insane*, woman?" Hook cried. "I've already lost *one* arm to that slinking, slithering assemblage of scales and teeth—I don't intend to lose *another*!"

"Oh, all right," the exasperated queen huffed. "Then *you* hold his mouth open and *I'll* do the work that needs to be done!"

Even this Hook was hesitant to do. But fearing the woman might leave him in the cave if he didn't (or worse—feed him to her newfound pet!), he steeled himself to the task. Sitting astraddle the crocodile's back, he grabbed the top of its snout with his one good hand and held the jaws open.

"Men," the queen sneered. "Ask them to do *one* little thing—like stick their arm down a crocodile's throat..." Lying down, she stuck her hand into the beast's mouth without hesitation.

"They're all such *babies*!"

Her face twisting in concentration, she began to fish about blindly inside the crocodile.

"A-*hah*!" she exclaimed at last, then withdrew her hand—to find that she was clutching a lady's silver hairbrush!

"We'll have to teach you not to put just *any* old thing in your mouth, my pretty," she mildly scolded the crocodile. Tossing the brush aside, she tried again.

In quick succession, she then extracted the following items from inside the reptile: a baby rattle, a sextant, a shoe (men's size eight and three-quarters) and a toy bugle.

"I'm not sure how much longer I can hold his jaws open," Hook gasped.

Sangramore merely scowled scornfully at him, then shoved her entire arm down the crocodile's gullet. This time, when she withdrew it her hand was grasping the annoying clock!

A deep, heavy, satisfied sigh escaped from the crocodile's innards; and once Hook released his jaw and rose off his back the beast rolled over and attempted to rub his now contented belly.

His short crocodilian legs made that virtually impossible—so Sangramore was kind enough to rub his tummy for him. From that moment on, the creature was completely devoted to the queen.

With Captain Hook's willing assistance, Sangramore had managed to recruit or Shanghai enough men to form a skeleton crew aboard the *Jolly Roger*, which she made her home and headquarters.

Having become rather intrigued by the much-touted Peter Pan, she began to spy on him secretly—sometimes by using her owl familiar, and sometimes by physically stalking the boy herself.

It was not long past that Mister Smee had shown up—having heard from his pirate brothers that Hook was alive and well.

Smee again offered his services to the captain—who counter-offered to hang Smee from the yardarm for spreading the lie that Hook was afraid of him!

That's when Smee counter-counter-offered to give Hook and the Queen of Diamonds a treasure in exchange for being accepted back into the fold.

Smee told them about obtaining the chest that held the first clue to the treasure's location—but he wouldn't reveal where, how or from whom, shivering and sweating from fear at the very thought and memory of these. Nor could he tell them what the purported treasure was, though surely it had to be something wonderful, else it wouldn't be a treasure.

He also admitted that he could not understand or unravel the meaning of the riddle contained inside the chest. As it turned out, neither could Hook, Sangramore or any of the other pirates. (Nor could the crocodile, of course.)

It was also Smee who suggested that Peter Pan—known as he was for his cleverness—just might be clever enough to decipher the riddle for them.

"After all—he was clever enough to defeat Cap'n Hook!" Smee said almost gleefully—then slapped both hands over his mouth a few words too late.

Hook wanted to throttle Smee for the very idea, but Queen Sangramore saw wisdom in the suggestion and thought it bore exploring.

The last time Sangramore had surreptitiously followed Pan he had made one of his periodic jaunts back to the Real World. He had led the queen to Kensington Square—where she noted that Pan seemed to be taking an inordinate interest in a certain little girl who appeared to have caught his fancy.

That girl, of course, had been Alice. Even though she had aged a few years since last she had wandered into the madness of Wonderland, Sangramore still recognized her.

That's when a marvelous plan had hatched, full-grown inside Sangramore's devious brain.

The evil queen stole into Alice's house that night, quietly exploring it from top to bottom before stealing into the girl's bedroom. Gambling that the child had grown older but not wiser and was still possessed of an unhealthy curiosity, Sangramore had whispered into Alice's ear, urging her to go to the attic.

During her earlier exploration, the queen had come upon the large looking glass and recognized it as being a potential portal that could be used to travel between worlds if only one knew how to use it—and Sangramore did.

That was how she got Alice to Neverland; she had manipulated the magical qualities of the mirror so that it would transport the girl there rather than back once more to Wonderland.

"But *why*?" Tinker Bell again insisted; she was rather peeved that her captor had told her everything *except* the answer to her initial question: Why had Sangramore brought Alice in to help carry out her plan to obtain the treasure?

"Isn't it obvious?" the queen said.

"Obviously not!" Tink replied.

The queen sighed and shook her head. "Taking you hostage would insure that Pan would be motivated to help us. But, for all his cleverness, Peter is a very flighty boy—literally and figuratively." She paused momentarily to giggle at her own pun.

"Let's face it; if left to his own devices, the poor scatterbrain just might get distracted and take off on an adventure of his own. Both you and the mission that should be occupying his every thought might instead fly right out of his skull!" She shook a finger at Tink.

"Do I lie?" she asked the fairy.

"No," Tink admitted, letting out a weary sigh. "You don't." She shrugged her tiny shoulders.

"Peter certainly means well, most of the time," she said. "But he has a brain like a dandelion. One strong puff of wind—and it scatters in a hundred different directions."

"Exactly," Sangramore concurred. "But I knew Alice would keep him focused and not let him stray too far from the straight and narrow."

"But what if she hadn't decided to go with him?" Tink asked.

"I'll admit, that was a possibility," Sangramore said. "But the little dimwit is such a *proper* young lady. And with that usually comes a sense of obligation toward others.

"Besides, what *else* did she have to do—sit around and play with fairies all day?"

"There are far *worse* ways to while away the hours," Tink said defensively.

"Not for a proper young lady there aren't," the queen rebuffed. She then spun on her heels and departed from the cabin, with the crocodile and Captain Hook right behind her.

"Oooh!" Tink stewed in frustration. She grabbed the bars of her cage and shook them with all her might, but they didn't budge.

"A question," Captain Hook asked of the queen as they walked away from the cabin. "If that blasted Pan *does* succeed in bringing us the treasure—"

"Bringing *me* the treasure," Sangramore corrected.

"Bringing *you* the treasure; you don't intend to just let him, the fairy and the little blonde trollop *go*, do you?"

"Of course not," the queen said coldly. "Alive and free, they could continue to be potential enemies." She smiled just as frigidly and stroked the pirate's cheek.

"*Dead…*they'll be nothing more than *memories!*"

Chapter 26

In the forest not far from where the Hangman's Tree had stood, Peter Pan awoke with a start.

It was fully dark now but he was lying inside the circle of light from a cheery campfire. He sat up a little too quickly, causing his head to swim and threatening to make him faint again. When he lifted a hand to his head, he saw that the upper part of his left arm was now bandaged.

As his vision cleared and his eyes once more focused, he saw Alice seated on the opposite side of the fire, smiling at him. Nor was she alone; a man was seated next her, also smiling.

The man looked to be incredibly old—at least 40. Black, high-topped patent leather shoes poked out from the bottoms of the legs of black-and-white checked trousers. The man also wore a black, Prince Albert coat over a brocaded vest and white shirt held closed at the collar by a large black bow tie. The fellow had long, thick, muttonchop sideburns and a bushy gray moustache below a slightly bulbous nose. A battered, black top hat sat at an angle atop his head.

The one part of his face that didn't seem old was his eyes, though there were little wrinkles at the corners of them. They were bright green with a bit of boyish sparkle to them.

"What happened?" Pan asked.

"It was horrible," Alice replied. "We were so caught up in celebrating our victory over the Hangman's Tree that neither of us noticed you have been *wounded!*" Pan's right hand touched the bandaged area on his arm and he winced.

"A large splinter of wood from the tree must have pierced your arm," Alice surmised. "And you bled so much you fainted dead away."

"And who is *he*?" Pan asked, pointing to the avuncular old man.

"Why, this is Mister Phineas Philogenias."

" BUT WHY ? "

"*Doctor* Philogenias," the man corrected.

"*Doctor* Philogenias," Alice corrected.

"I've had no experience at all with treating wounds," she continued, "and was at a total loss as to what I should do when you passed out.

"Luckily for both of us, Doctor Philogenias came riding along at just that very moment."

As she spoke, a rather scruffy looking, little, gray donkey stepped into the light of the fire. It nudged the old man with its nose and in response Philogenias pulled a bit of carrot from a coat pocket. The placid donkey ate it right out of his hand.

"This is Doctor Philogenias' noble steed," Alice said rather grandly. "His name is Footloose."

"How do you do?" Pan said, then motioned with one hand.

"Go on with the story," he prompted.

"Where was I?" Alice said. "Oh. Oh, yes. Well, the good doctor removed the remnants of wood from your arm, cleaned out the wound thoroughly and then stitched it up neater than a Savoy Row tailor!"

"And what about the bandage?" Peter asked. "Something about it looks a bit familiar."

The light cast off by the fire was sufficient for him to see that Alice was again blushing. She tugged at her tattered dress as if trying to make sure it covered everything sufficiently.

"Yes, well." It was the old man who spoke now, in a melodious, singsong voice. "I'm afraid I am currently running a bit low on proper bandaging material.

"Fortunately, the young lady here was graciously willing to sacrifice some of the material from her *petticoat* to serve that function!"

Seeing Peter smile at this, Alice moaned and buried her face in her hands.

"But I *do* have plenty of *this*!" the self-proclaimed "doctor" exclaimed, pulling a small bottle out of yet another of his coat pockets. The glass container was filled with a reddish black liquid and bore a label covered with such fine print that Pan would have had difficulty making all the words out even if he *could* read.

"And what exactly *is* this, you may rightly ask," Philogenias went on, speaking just as loudly as if he had an audience of a hundred rather than just two children and a donkey.

"This, ladies and gentlemen—er, lady and gentleman...and you, too, of course, Footloose...this is nothing less than a bottle of Dr. Phineas Philogenias' Florid Flagon of Phantasmagorical and Fortitudinous Fortifying Fluid!

"Patent pending."

Alice and Pan sat transfixed. Neither had ever heard such a tidal wave of alliterative acumen flow forth in a single breath.

Recognizing that he now had a captive audience, Philogenias plunged onward.

"Of what does this wondrous potion consist, you might also ask," (though it was he himself who was doing all the asking).

"Alas, the list of ingredients to be found inside each and every bottle is a closely guarded trade secret known only to a smidgen of shamans, a modicum of mystics, a few pharmacists—and me, Dr. Phineas Philogenias: MD, DO, PhD, DDS and DMV. And when required, Notary Public."

The two children were greatly impressed.

"Suffice it to say," Philogenias declared, "that this patent panacea has been proven anecdotally to cure piles, shingles, hives, gout, hair loss, lumbago, maladies of both the upper and lower intestine and of the inner and outer heart, flat feet, billiousness and crossed eyes.

"But surely, you must also be asking right about now, a bottle of such a miraculous maledictum must surely cost a veritable king's ransom.

"And you would be right!" This last bit was barked out so loudly that Alice nearly toppled over.

"But I like you two youngsters," Philogenias continued in a softer tone, smiling warmly at both of them. "You've got *spunk*—the one thing my exquisite elixir *won't* eliminate!

"So, for you and you alone, today and today only, I am willing—nay, happy—to part with a bottle of my Fortifying Fluid for the ridiculously low price of *one dollar*!" He gave each of them a wink.

"Feel free to purchase multiple bottles. Offer good while supplies last."

The snake oil salesman glanced eagerly from one to the other of them but each looked back slightly shamefaced.

"I'm afraid I didn't think to bring any money with me when I left the house," Alice confessed, "since I didn't really know I *would* be leaving the house. What about you, Peter?"

"Not a farthing," the boy said (not thinking of the piece of eight dangling from his ear). "I've never had much need for money here in Neverland."

Dr. Philogenias sighed and shrugged. "It was worth a shot," he said. "I guess Footloose and I shall be on our way, then."

"Oh, no, doctor," Alice said. "At least stay till morning; we'd be more than happy to share our foodstuff with you this evening."

"I thank you, child. And I'm sure Footloose thanks you, too. But we have miles to go, patients to see and elixir to sell." For emphasis, he popped the cork on the bottle of "medicine" in his hand and took a generous swallow himself.

"What about Peter's arm?" Alice asked.

"It should be fine," Philogenias assured her. "Just keep the stitched area cleaned and put a fresh bandage on it every day for a few days." He took another large gulp of elixir, then eyed her closely.

"Have you still got plenty of petticoat?"

"I believe so," she replied abashedly, casting her eyes down modestly.

"Then I bid you farewell," Philogenias said. First, though, he tipped the bottle to his lips once more.

After several loud gulps, he eyed the bottle quizzically. It seemed to surprise him that it was now empty; but he shrugged philosophically and tossed it away.

For some reason, Alice wasn't sure why, the doctor staggered a bit as he walked to where Footloose patiently waited. When his first two attempts to mount the donkey failed, Alice rushed over to give him a boost on his third try.

This time he succeeded, though he doubtless would have fallen right off had not Alice supplied a steadying hand. The old man took a deep breath, then looked down at the girl. Smiling paternally, he lightly stroked her cheek with one hand.

He reached into a pack slung over his donkey's back and pulled out a small bundle wrapped in oilskin.

"Here's a little bit of jerked meat," he said, handing the bundle to Alice. "Give it to the boy; it'll help him replace the blood he's lost."

"Thank you very much, doctor," Alice said gratefully.

"You children be careful," Philogenias said with slightly slurred speech. "The world can be a dangerous place."

"We will be, doctor," Alice replied. "And you be careful, too."

"I shall be, Alice. Never fear." He tapped his donkey lightly in the sides with his heels. "*On*, Footloose!"

As the faux physician and his steed disappeared into the darkness, Alice could hear the old man's voice raised in song, though she could make out only a few of the words.

Something about a sailor and a woman named Sal.

A romantic ballad, no doubt.

Chapter 27

"H e's an odd fellow," Pan observed after Dr. Philogenias had vanished into the night.

"Says the boy who never grew up and who lives in a land of fairies and mermaids," Alice teased.

"Well, yes…but they're not *odd* fairies and mermaids!"

"That odd fellow may just have saved your life, Mister Pan—so I guess not all grown-ups are useless."

"I don't believe I ever specifically said they *all* were," Pan dissembled. "Just most of them."

"And you still don't want to *be* one."

"Heavens no!" Pan declared, as adamant as ever. "And by now, *you* shouldn't want to be one, either!"

"Whatever do you mean?"

"I mean it's been fun being free with me these last few days, hasn't it?"

"Fun?" Alice exclaimed. "*Fun*? Only if you think that being chased by serpents, almost being eaten by Yeti and nearly being hanged *fun*!"

"But it *is*, though, just a bit—isn't it?" Pan replied with that wily and nearly irresistible smile he had.

Alice scowled silently at him for a moment. Then, 'neath the warmth of that smile of his, her features softened. She, too, smiled—then laughed.

"You know," she admitted, "it really rather *has* been!"

Feeling compelled to behave maturely, however, she then affected a look of mock seriousness and wagged a scolding finger at Peter.

"But don't delude yourself for one minute, Mister Pan, into believing that you don't also on occasion behave just like a grown-up!"

"I do *not*!" he protested vehemently. "You take that back!"

"I will not," she said stubbornly. "And I can *prove* it!"

"By all means do so, then," Pan snapped. He leaned back against a fallen tree trunk, then bit off and began to chew furiously at a piece of the tough meat Dr. Philogenias had left for him.

"All right," Alice said firmly. "But just remember that you asked for it." She sat and collected her thoughts for a minute before continuing.

"Two examples come to mind immediately," she began. "The first is when you did not hesitate for the blink of an eye to agree to do whatever was required to save your dear Tink.

"Then there was the moment when you chose not to leave me alone on the raft, even though you could easily have flown away to safety and found somebody else who could have read the riddle for you." She smiled to soften the blow of what she was about to say next.

"I would say that both of those actions were the result of very, very grown-up decisions. Wouldn't you?"

At the very thought, Pan sat silently pouting and slowly chewing his meat for quite some time.

"Nonetheless," he said at last, "you have to admit that it is certainly more fun to be a child than it is to be a grown-up."

"I suppose I do," Alice did indeed admit. She then found herself growing somewhat melancholy.

"But just about everything that's waiting for me back home is incredibly grown-up," she said sadly.

"Then, just don't go back there!" was Pan's nonchalant recommendation.

Alice sighed. "What about you, Peter? Once this is all over and Tink is safe and sound…what do you intend to do next?"

"I hadn't really thought about it," he said, biting off another piece of jerked meat. (He couldn't tell just what sort of animal this meat had come from, and suspected it might be best that he didn't know!)

"Maybe I'll try to find *Foreverland*," he told Alice.

"Foreverland," the girl replied almost wistfully. "What's that?"

"I'm sure I don't know," Pan replied.

"Then why would you want to go there?"

Pan chuckled. "Well, now, if I already knew what was there—there wouldn't be much point in going there, would there?"

"I'm not sure that's entirely true," Alice replied. "After all, I know what's in Italy—but I'd still like to go there and see it with my own eyes. But I see your point. Is there anything you *do* know about it?"

"The legends about Foreverland are pretty vague," he told her, "but they all hint that it is one of the most incredible places imaginable. I'd certainly like to find out for myself whether that's true or not." In one of those rare moments, this boy who refused to grow up became serious.

"It would almost certainly have to be better than some of the places I've been."

"What sort of places, Peter?" Alice asked softly. He stared at her intently for the longest of times, as if weighing his words carefully before replying. When he did speak, it was in such a low and somber tone that Alice had to strain to hear him.

"Like the place where the souls of dead children go," he said darkly.

"*Oh!*" Alice cried out, horrified by the very thought that there could ever be such a place. But she was curious, too.

"Tell me about it, Peter."

"Are you sure?"

"Please."

He sat staring at the leaping flames of their campfire for several moments before he began.

"It's a gloomy, shadowy place," he told her. "Filled with sadness. The darkness never ends and there is always a sound like the wind through the trees, though no matter where you go the sound seems to be coming from far away."

"How did you ever find such a place?" Alice asked breathlessly.

"It's not so much that I found it," Peter replied. "It's more like I was simply drawn there one day. How or why, I've never known.

"As near as I can tell, the souls of dead children almost always go straight-away to the light that then carries them to their final home. It happens the very moment they stop breathing.

"But sometimes—not very often, but sometimes—one of those poor little souls gets lost. I don't know why; maybe because its life was taken too soon or too suddenly. Or too horribly." He then managed a little smile.

"Or perhaps it just really, really, really didn't want to go at all."

"And what's it like there…for *you*?" Alice asked, enthralled by his story.

Peter closed his eyes. "I had flown for a long time, that first time I went there, without knowing why. Now, when the call comes, I always recognize it. I imagine there are places on the moon that look something like it, all dead and lifeless.

"There are no trees there, no sign of birds or animals. Everything looks gray, and the darkness never ends.

"A fog that seems to flow through you as well as around you is always present. Shadows move in and out of the fog, though you can't see anything that would cast a shadow.

"It's so quiet that you can hear your heartbeat, yet at the same time you seem to hear a constant sound, like people who are far away, crying.

"There seemed to be nothing at all there, so I was prepared to just turn around and leave. Then I heard a voice.

"It was the most eerie thing I had ever heard. Otherworldly, as if it was almost but not quite human. Part of me wanted to run away from it."

"I do believe that's exactly what I would have done," Alice interjected.

Pan shook his head. "But a greater part of me was drawn to the sound of it. The fog grew thicker, until I could barely see well enough to place one foot in front of the other. Yet with each of those steps, the voice that had called out to me grew a little louder, a littler clearer.

"'Can you help me'?" it said.

"From somewhere out of the fog and the dark, a small figure appeared, slowly walking toward me. It was a little girl, no more than five years old.

"Like everything in that place, she had no real color to her at all. Just a sort of grayness. And she had eyes that spoke of great sorrow.

"In that very instant, I just instinctively knew the truth about her; I don't know how. By delaying its final journey, the soul of this poor child had become lost and could no longer find its way to the light alone.

"'If you'd like,' I said, 'I could be your guide and your companion, and help you get to where you need to be'—for somehow I just knew I could indeed do this. 'I can get you to the happy place.'

"Those hollow, empty eyes of hers grew bigger and she stepped back as if she were afraid of me or afraid of the journey."

"What did you do, what did you say to convince that poor little angel to follow you?" Alice asked, dabbing at tears in both eyes.

Peter looked up at the stars. "I told her that to die and be truly dead… was an awfully big adventure.

"I knew that almost all children—even ones that are no longer alive—like to go on adventures!

"Then I held out my hand to her." As if to illustrate, Pan stretched one hand toward the campfire.

"Finally, she reached out with her own little hand. It was cold and waxy to the touch at first, but it seemed to absorb some of the warmth from my own. I looked up from it and saw that tears were flowing down both of the little girl's cheeks."

(The same was now true of Alice.)

"And then you took her to her eternal home?"

"Not all the way, no," Pan replied, seeming to shiver slightly. "I only take these souls close enough to the light that they can then find their own way onward. I admit, I've always been a little afraid that if I got too close to the light myself—I might be drawn into it, too!"

He chuckled softly. "That's one adventure I'm not quite ready to embark on just yet!" He then grew serious.

"I've helped others since that first little girl," he said. "Boys and girls of all ages. Even little babies too young to know they were lost." An expression resembling anger twisted his features.

"Some were there because *grown-ups* had done…horrible…unspeakable things to them. Instead of caring for them…they had condemned them to a journey no child should have to make."

"How sad," Alice sobbed. "For them *and* for you." She reached out and ran a comforting hand along Pan's arm.

"But how *wonderful*, too. Without you to guide them, Peter, those poor, lost little souls might be trapped in the shadows forever!"

"I suppose." Pan was beginning to wish he had never told Alice about this part of his life. But he had; and her curiosity about it was understandable.

"And you still have no idea *why* it was you who was called upon to perform this duty?"

"None."

"Nor who it is that chose you and informs you when you're needed?"

"No."

Alice pondered this for a moment. "And when you receive one of these calls…could you choose not to respond, not to go to that terrible place?"

"I suppose I could."

"But you never do, do you?"

"No."

"Why not? Forgive my boldness, but why do you allow yourself to be put through such obvious torment?"

He chuckled without humor. "Torment? What is *my* pain when placed alongside that of some poor little boy or girl who's out there lost in the darkness? Alone, confused, helpless. What would become of them if I wasn't there to show them the way?"

"You don't think some *other* guide would be chosen to do that job?"

"I don't know. Maybe. But I can't be sure. All I *do* know is that it's the duty of *each* child to try to help every *other* child. We can't always count on grown-ups to do it." Again she heard bitterness in his usually cheerful voice.

"But those little lost souls will always be able to count on *me*!"

After that, she and Pan simply sat together in awkward silence for a spell. Then Peter straightened up and slapped both knees.

"What say we open our latest chest and see where the riddle is going to take us?"

"Oh, let's," Alice concurred. She opened the box, removed the scroll contained therein and began to read.

Two cats in houses made of skins.
One born of love, one born of sin.

Mark the spot where the black cat falls,
And there you'll find the final call.

As always, it took Pan but a moment to decipher the meaning of the riddle, and the answer made him perk up and smile.

"At last," he said, "a riddle that's going to send us to a *happy* place!"

"Where's that?" Alice inquired.

"The answer has to be the Indian village!" Pan declared.

"Indians?" Alice said. "*Red* Indians? Like they have in the Americas?"

"I don't know about the Americas," Pan said. "But they're the only Indians we have in Neverland. And this time, we should have no difficulty at all."

"Why not?"

"Because the Indians *love* me!" Pan crowed.

Chapter 28

"I hate Peter Pan! I want to *kill* him!"

These threatening, venomous words spewed from the lips of the Indian warrior called Little Panther. He was addressing that sentiment to a pirate called Starkey, who (aside from Mister Smee) was the only surviving member of Captain Hook's original crew.

Since the crushing defeat at the hands of Peter Pan and his Lost Boys, Starkey had lived quietly among the Indians. Relegated to helping care for their children, he seemed to be a man who was completely cowed.

But appearances can be deceiving (as your mother has probably already taught you). At heart (which is where it most matters), Starkey was still very much and thoroughly a blackguard. He had long been using his piratical wiles to ingratiate himself to and influence Little Panther.

This had proven to be a surprisingly easy task to accomplish. Little Panther was already filled with hate and resentment, and such people often prove quite easy to manipulate.

Little Panther believed that, by being the acknowledged best hunter and greatest warrior in the tribe, he was entitled to receive two rewards: the title of *chief*—and the beautiful *Tiger Lily* as his *wife*.

The current chief of the tribe—Tiger Lily's father, Man Alone—believed his people should live in peace and focus on the twin skills of hunting and gathering fruits and vegetables.

Such pursuits, to Little Panther's way of thinking, were fine—for women. But he preferred to follow the ways of war and believed his tribe should use their power to conquer and control all of Neverland.

Already, this philosophical difference of opinion had caused a schism within the tribe.

The main body of the village, under the leadership of Man Alone, was situated in a part of the northwest region of Neverland, not far inland from the sea.

But a short, narrow isthmus connected the mainland there to a small outcropping of land no more than a few hundred feet in diameter. Both it and the land bridge also stood a good hundred feet above the normal level of the water below. To show he was distancing himself from the rest of the people, Little Panther had erected his lodge there.

A dozen or more other warriors, mostly young, had joined Little Panther, setting up their lodges in a circle around his. They acknowledged him as their leader and shared his dream of conquest. Tensions were mounting daily between them and the members of the main body of the tribe.

This was the situation when Pan and Alice walked into the village, neither of them aware of the dire situation.

Word went out quickly that Peter had returned, and men, women and children (and even a few of the village dogs) rushed to greet him. He laughed and they laughed with him, hugging him and slapping him on the back (for aside from Little Panther, Starkey and perhaps a few of Little Panther's followers, the people of the village truly *did* love the boy!).

Alice hung back shyly (and a little bit fearfully). She had never seen such people before save in her own imagination and a book she had read, written by an American named James Fenimore Cooper.

The people in whose midst she now found herself reminded her of some of those who inhabited Cooper's rousing adventure tale; and she found herself wondering if it was possible that they belonged to some lost tribe of the Iroquois Confederation that had somehow come to dwell in Neverland. Several of them wore the coif described in the book: their heads shaved bare but for a strip right down the middle.

To her proper Victorian eyes they did seem to be shamefully immodest. The men were practically naked, their exposed flesh glistening with oil; some of the very youngest children were *totally* naked. Nor did the women seem to wear much more than did the men. Alice didn't know where to look, for everywhere she turned her eyes fell upon something she felt no young lady should see.

A voice called out a command in a loud tone that made Alice jump with surprise and the crowd surrounding her and Pan grew slightly quieter and parted like the waters of the Red Sea before the staff of Moses.

The man they had all made way for was an older gentleman, tall and erect. Though Alice didn't know it yet, this was Man Alone, longtime chief of the tribe. Stately in appearance, he walked slowly toward the two children.

As he drew close, another Indian who had been walking out of sight behind the chief stepped into view and Alice's breath caught in her bosom.

She felt certain this could be none other than *Tiger Lily*, daughter of the chief. Peter had spoken of her to Alice, but had failed to mention how stunningly *beautiful* she was.

A man whose way with words far surpassed my own once described Tiger Lily as being "proudly erect, a princess in her own right. She is the most beautiful of dusky Dianas."

At the moment of first meeting her, Alice would have felt that author to be guilty of gross understatement.

Though of nearly the same age as Alice, Tiger Lily stood at least two inches taller. Her almond colored skin was flawless. Her dark eyes were slightly slanted in an exotic fashion, her lips full and pouty and colored with the juice of some bright berry.

Her hair was black as coal and hung nearly to her waist. A round, color-fully beaded ornament was attached on one side of her head, with two red hawk feathers hanging from it.

"Welcome back, Peter," was all she said, but the warmth exuded by those three words could have melted an iceberg.

As if a dam had burst, the people again set up a cheer and swarmed back over Pan, drawing him to the center of the village.

The rise of land attached to the isthmus, upon which sat the enclave of rebel Indians, stood slightly higher than the mainland and thus offered an unobstructed view of the main village. It was from here that the hate-filled Little Panther had seen the arrival of Peter Pan and it was because of this that he had uttered the venomous words speaking of his desire to see the boy dead.

"I've no love for the scoundrel, either," the pirate Starkey replied.

"Then you can help me kill him!" Little Panther snarled.

Starkey wasn't at all sure he wanted to do that. Oh, to be sure, he didn't mind engaging in a bit of murder, especially for profit; he was, after all, still at heart a pirate in good standing. But when dealing with one as slippery as Peter Pan, there was great risk that *you* might end up being the murder*ee* rather than the murder*er*.

"Let's think this over carefully, chief," Starkey said slyly, stroking Little Panther's ego by using the honorific when addressing him.

"Which is more important: Killing Pan...or claiming Tiger Lily and becoming chief of all the tribe?"

So strong was his hatred for Pan that Little Panther had to think long and hard on this.

In truth, the ill will he harbored toward Pan was mostly fueled by *envy*. The villagers all loved the happy, jovial boy, who often earned their affection through unselfish acts of kindness. They held no such warmth in their hearts for the cold and aloof Little Panther.

Then there was the matter of the lovely Tiger Lily. Every brave in the village would love to have her for one of his wives. So far, however, she had warded off any amorous advances—with a brandished tomahawk if necessary.

But Pan, Little Panther knew, would meet no such resistance from the girl; she thought the sun, moon and stars were all hung in the heavens to honor him.

Little Panther hated Peter most of all for this.

While the self-absorbed warrior stewed in his own jealous juices, the men and women of the main village set about preparing for a large celebration in light of Peter Pan's return to their midst.

(Indians—like most people, most times and most places—were always looking for *some* cause to celebrate!)

As was their custom, they built a large bonfire in the center of the village. Numerous platters of food were passed around by the women, containing roasted venison and various roots and vegetables.

At some point, the music began. Some men pounded in rhythm on certain types of drums while others kept the beat on flutes and whistles.

And what would music be if it did not breed dancing? Two circles of dancers formed around the fire: women in the inner circle, men in the outer circle. In step with each other, each circle would move toward the other, then back before stepping to one side so that the two circles seemed to revolve around the fire.

Tiger Lily broke away from the other women, who closed ranks, then passed through the outer circle of dancing men to the place where her father Man Alone sat with Peter Pan and Alice. The chief was smiling and bobbing his head at the dancers.

"Join us!" Tiger Lily said to Peter, grabbing his hands and pulling him to his feet. He was happy to do so.

"Come with us!" he said to Alice, holding out one hand. She laughed but vigorously shook her head and waved him away; to behave with such wild abandon as the dancers was exhibiting was foreign to Alice's experience and disposition. Pan shrugged and moved toward the circle of dancers.

Just short of reaching the outer band, he let out an enthusiastic whoop and leaped into the air. He flew over both circles of dancers, executed a perfect somersault in midair and landed lightly right next to the bonfire.

"*Yeee-Haaa!*" he screeched at the top of his lungs, and all the dancers echoed his gleeful cry.

With joyful fervor, Pan once again displayed his prowess as a dancer. He hopped and skipped, leaped and wheeled. The music began to play faster and he sped up his steps to match it. As the drumming and the piping reached a crescendo, Peter leaped straight up into the air, higher than the flames of the bonfire.

His arms and legs shot out to both sides and he again loosed a loud yowl. When he plunged back to earth, he landed on one knee with his head bowed. When he raised it, he began to laugh, then whooped and howled at the moon as he danced around anew.

Raising their arms to the sky, the men and women circling around Pan gave an answering shout. Then they, too, began to dance as wildly as this free spirit in their midst.

Alice too laughed and clapped her hands. Turning her head, she saw Chief Man Alone looking at her. A wide smile turned up the corners of his mouth and deepened the wrinkles around his friendly eyes. He jerked his head in the direction of the dancers.

Deciding that dancing was more desirous than was decorum, Alice cast her inhibitions aside, jumped to her feet and joined the others. Within moments, she, Tiger Lily and Peter were all holding hands and dancing about wildly.

What would the people back home have thought had they seen this proper young lady hopping and spinning like a dervish and howling at the moon like a wild wolf?

In the moment, Alice couldn't have cared less.

The people of the village continued their celebration till well into the night: dancing and eating, eating and dancing.

Only when the bonfire began to die down did the villagers begin to drift toward their homes and their beds. And only then did Alice notice that Peter's face looked rather pale and that perspiration wetly plastered down his hair against the sides of his flushed face.

"You pushed yourself too hard," she said, moving close to Pan's side and putting her arm around his waist. "It's too soon; you haven't fully healed yet."

"Nonsense," the boy insisted, though he was breathing a little harder than normal. "A good party with good music, good food and good people is the best medicine of all!"

"As is a good night's sleep," Alice scolded mildly.

"She's right," Tiger Lily said, coming up on Peter's other side when she saw his feet were dragging and putting her arm around him as well.

They assisted him in reaching the large lodge of Chief Man Alone and laid him (though he resisted) on a bed of thick, soft bearskin. He fell asleep almost as soon as his head came to rest.

Alice and Tiger Lily, being neither so drained nor so tired as was Pan, stayed up a while longer, sitting by the small, comforting fire in the center of the lodge and talking. From the inside, Alice now got her best view of how the Indians' dwellings were constructed.

Several saplings had been placed in the ground in a circle. The saplings were bent over and fastened together where they converged, creating a curved framework. Depending upon the size of the structure, a dozen or more tanned animal skins were then stretched over this framework to create a rounded dwelling. As might be expected, the lodge of Man Alone was the largest in the village.

Alice told the Indian maiden the story of how she came to be in Neverland and of the quest she and Pan were on to save Tinker Bell.

Tiger Lily shook her head. "We've had our village here for quite some time," she told Alice. "But I've never seen anything like the boxes you described."

"That's all right," Alice said. "I'm sure it's somewhere near here. We'll find it."

"Yes," Tiger Lily said, gazing over at the sleeping Pan. "I believe Peter can do anything he sets his mind to."

For some reason she couldn't have explained, the way Tiger Lily looked at the slumbering boy bothered Alice in ever so slight a way.

"Have you known him for a long time?" she asked.

"All my life, it seems," Tiger Lily replied. "For I was someone else when we first met."

"Tell me about that," Alice said.

"Oh, it's late, Alice. You don't want to stay up listening to my story."

"But I *do*!"

Tiger Lily smiled in remembrance. "Well, it *is* quite a tale, if I do say so myself.

"You see, the day I met Peter Pan—was also the day we both almost *died*!"

"ALICE COULDN'T HAVE CARED LESS."

Chapter 29

Among certain tribes of Indians, including the ones who dwelt in Neverland, it was not uncommon for a person to have one name when they were a child—and a different name entirely when they grew up.

So it was with Tiger Lily. When she was but a little girl, she was known as *Daybreak*. As lovely then as she was now, she was also a very curious child, possessed with a great love of flowers.

She happened to hear others talking about a place not far from where the Indian village was then located: a place said to be filled with the loveliest flowers that ever grew in the world.

This place was rumored to be not far from the Mermaids' Lagoon. At that time, Daybreak had never seen a mermaid, so naturally her curiosity was greatly aroused.

Unfortunately, the place where the flowers grew was also one of the most *dangerous* spots imaginable: filled with fearsome predators who would just as soon gobble up a little Indian girl as they would a Christmas goose! So Daybreak's father, the wise Chief Man Alone, sternly forbade his precious daughter to go anywhere near there.

Having never heard the saying that curiosity killed the cat, and being almost as brave as a full-grown woman, Daybreak picked a morning when she knew her father and many of the other men would be away hunting and sneaked out of the village unobserved.

After walking for a few hours, and having neglected to fortify herself with any breakfast before setting out from the village, Daybreak began to wonder if the place of flowers really existed at all or if it was just a myth.

But just as she was about to give up and return to her village (and the inevitable scolding she was bound to receive from her protective father), she stumbled upon the fabled primordial garden.

The stories she had heard had not been sufficient to adequately prepare her for what she beheld. In an open area larger than Trafalgar Square, wild flowers of every description grew in epic abundance. Almost any species you'd care to name was represented here: roses, daffodils, sunflowers, gardenias, orchids, azaleas and petunias. Flowers that ordinarily would never grow together in the same spot were growing here in harmony, side-by-side.

Including *lilies*.

Those were Daybreak's favorite flowers of all. The ones growing in a patch here were all of purest white, their petals as bright as the snow.

Daybreak had never seen anything as beautiful as this little piece of Paradise and all its flowery inhabitants.

(That was actually not true, for the girl saw something just as lovely—maybe even *more* lovely—every time she gazed at her own reflection in a pool of water. Such was the genuine modesty of this dark maiden, though, that such a thought would have found no purchase inside her mind.)

For a time, Daybreak simply lay on her back in the middle of the flower field; staring up at the clouds and letting the multitude of floral fragrances wash over her. Not far away, a small, racing waterfall rose thirty feet into the air, spilling its contents into a babbling brook that ran near where the girl reclined.

Almost intoxicated by the odors of nature enveloping her, Daybreak next went to kneel amidst a patch of the lovely lilies. As she picked a few of the blossoms and began weaving them into her lustrous hair, she softly sang a song her mother had taught her.

Some see only land and sky,
The things that crawl and the things that fly.
But you must look with more than eye.
If you look instead with all your heart,
And see worlds end and see worlds start,
You'll know all things...and know your part.

Daybreak stopped singing in order to listen, for she thought for just a moment that she had heard the sound of other voices: also singing, but a different song. It was as if she was hearing some sort of heavenly choir.

Almost mesmerized by the chorus, the girl crawled on hands and knees in the direction from which the singing appeared to be coming. She gasped softly as she quietly pushed aside some bull rushes and found herself looking out over a sparkling blue lagoon.

Atop some of the rocks dotting the lagoon were half a dozen of the mermaids for whom the spot was named!

Daybreak knew about the mermaids but this was the very first time she actually laid eyes upon them. She was instantly enthralled, thinking that their beauty might even surpass that of the field of flowers.

The song they sang seemed to have no actual words to it, yet still it spoke to Daybreak of many things: of sorrow and longing, but also of joy and a tempting promise of love.

So entranced was she by their singing and their loveliness that Daybreak failed to hear a rustling in the rushes behind her or a low, guttural growling.

It was only when the growl became a full-throated *roar* that she was pulled from her reverie—turning her head in time to see a fully-grown *tiger* charging toward her!

The tiger leaped. Daybreak screamed. The startled mermaids all fearfully plunged beneath the waters of the lagoon.

And then a laughing boy, dressed only in skeleton leaves, came plummeting down out of the sky!

Peter Pan (for, of course, that's who the flying boy was) landed atop the hungry tiger's back while it was still in mid-leap. His added weight caused the beast to crash to the ground, no more than two strides away from the dumbfounded Daybreak.

The tiger shrieked in a tigerish way and began to twist and buck like an untamed bronco; but the boy had grabbed two hands full of the furry ruff around its head and clamped his knees tightly against its sides. All the while the boy laughed as if he was having great fun.

Daybreak could do nothing but watch in amazement as beast and boy rolled, tumbled and plunged out of sight into a large canebrake.

The girl lost sight of the combatants but could hear the sounds of their continuing struggle and see by the swaying and swishing of the cane roughly where they were as they thrashed about. The cane grew on a slope that angled up toward the nearby waterfall and their fight seemed to be carrying them up toward that small cataract.

Daybreak followed from below as best she could, on a path that led her away from the lagoon and back toward the brook below the falls.

Moments later, all sound and movement within the canebrake ceased. Daybreak held her breath and peered upward, wondering if both cat and boy had perished in their struggle.

"*Aaah!*" she cried, jumping in fearful startlement as the tiger unleashed a yowling roar. It then came crashing into view—bounding out of the cane in a mighty leap that took it out and over the edge of the waterfall.

"*Waaa-Hooo!*" shouted the boy gleefully. He was still riding atop the tiger, with one hand waving wildly in the air.

As the tiger's leap carried it through the air, though, the boy released his hold on it. The tiger's momentum continued to carry it forward, but the boy remained behind, hovering safely in midair.

The next battle the tiger lost was the one against gravity, as it began to fall. All four of its paws flailed wildly, but they could not prevent the beast from plummeting downward like a striped rock. It struck the surface of the brook belly first and disappeared in a huge spray of water.

Seconds later the tiger bobbed back to the surface and furiously paddled its way to shore—to the bank opposite the one on which stood the stunned Daybreak. Thoroughly chastised, the beast pulled itself out of the water, shook itself mightily, and then fled back into the forest.

"*That* was fun!" a cheerful voice called down to Daybreak. The triumphant flying boy fluttered down to earth in front of the Indian maiden.

"I'm Peter Pan," he said. "What's your name?"

The girl had a hard time making more than a squeak come out of her mouth but at last she was able to introduce herself.

"Daybreak," the boy repeated, gazing at her intently. "That's a pretty name."

"You're pretty, too," she blurted, then loudly sucked in air as if trying to pull back her impetuous declaration. Pan simply threw his head back and laughed merrily, and the girl found herself laughing along with him.

"You really *should* be more careful, though," Pan admonished, though not with any aspect of the scold about him. "There's nothing a tiger likes more than pouncing on someone while they're not looking."

"I'll remember that," she promised.

"See that you do," he replied, playfully wagging one finger at her. "I might not be around to help you the next time!"

"I don't know about that," Daybreak said, and the way she looked at him made him feel a little odd and tingly.

"Something tells me that whenever I might need you—you'll be there."

"I hope you're right," Pan said, smiling brightly.

"You've got to come back to my village with me," she again spoke impulsively.

"I'm not sure I should," Pan said hesitantly, taking a step back away from the girl. (At this time, he was not quite as confident and comfortable in the company of groups of others as he was now.)

"But you *must!*" Daybreak insisted, reaching out and grabbing hold of his hand. "They'll *all* want to meet you; I just *know* they will!"

Pan still had his doubts, but they diminished greatly in the warmth of Daybreak's hand around his. She maintained her hold on it for a long time after they left the field of flowers.

Everyone in the Indian village was astounded when, not long after, their princess returned to them, carrying with her an armload of white lilies and accompanied by this lovely, lively lad.

It was because of this adventure that Daybreak's father Man Alone then gave her a new name: *Tiger Lily*. (Though sometimes, when they were alone together, Pan still called her Daybreak.)

"From that day forward," Tiger Lily told Alice, "I, my father and most of the villagers have felt indebted to Peter."

("It's more than mere indebtedness she feels for him," Alice thought, seeing the way Tiger Lily looked at the slumbering Pan.)

As if unconsciously aware that he was being talked about, Peter began to twitch and mumble even as he slept. At one point, he could be heard to murmur aloud the single word "mother."

"Poor Peter," Alice said softly. "He must miss his mother terribly." She couldn't help but think of how greatly she missed her own.

Tiger Lily sighed sadly. "I don't believe he ever even *knew* his mother."

"But he's *told* me about her!" Alice objected.

"About how beautiful she was, yes?" Tiger Lily said. "And how she kissed him and loved him so much?"

"Well, yes," Alice said somewhat hesitantly. "And about his father, too."

"Yes," Tiger Lily replied, nodding her head. "He's told many stories, especially about his mother…but some contradict others he's told."

Alice was shocked. "You don't mean he *lied*?"

"Oh, no," Tiger Lily was quick to respond. "Peter *never* lies. He just…he just plays make believe. He plays it really well. So well that, sometimes, he's not sure himself what is make believe and what is real." She smiled slightly.

"He's just a boy, after all."

"Yes," Alice agreed. "One who insists on staying so forever."

Tiger Lily rose, walked over and knelt down beside Peter. With one hand she lightly stroked his hair in an effort to soothe his troubled sleep.

"Who can blame him?" she said softly, then looked back at Alice. "Did you know he still has his first teeth?"

"I'm sure I didn't," Alice replied.

"At times, before you came along," Tiger Lily said with just a mild edge to her voice, "he had his own little band of *Lost Boys* that he was the 'father' to.

"They may really have been lost; I don't know for sure. But I don't think Peter was a lost boy."

The flickering flames of the campfire seemed to sparkle off of Tiger Lily's eyes, and Alice realized this twinkling was the reflection of *tears*.

"I think he was an *unwanted* boy."

"Whatever does that mean?" Alice asked. Being a very proper young lady who had grown up within a very proper household inside a very proper community, the thing of which Tiger Lily spoke was totally alien to her.

"I think Peter's mother gave him away when he was just a baby," Tiger Lily said, herself almost choking on the words.

Alice gasped. "Why on earth would anyone *do* such a thing?"

"They wouldn't—in my world," Tiger Lily said. "But my world is very small. It consists mostly of just my village. And we all take care of each other.

"But Peter tells me *your* world is very big, Alice. Is that true?"

Alice had never really thought of that, but now she did. "I suppose it is," she said. "There are probably many more people living in my—my 'village'—than there are in all of Neverland."

"Then it must be very easy for someone to get lost there...or to be abandoned."

"I'm afraid that's true," Alice admitted. "But, still..."

"Maybe Peter's mother had no choice," Tiger Lily speculated. "Maybe his father was dead...and his mother was all alone and unable to care for him."

The concept, the very idea of someone being "alone" in a city the size of London had never before occurred to Alice; but she had to concede that it was possible.

"I think that may be one of the reasons he continues to go back to your world from time to time," Tiger Lily went on.

"I think a part of him believes—or at least wants to believe—that some day he and his mother will bump into each other. That each of them will magically recognize the other—and they will be a *real* mother and son again."

"Oh, dear," Alice moaned. "Oh, dear, dear, dear." Now she too could feel tears beginning to well up in her eyes.

"The poor baby."

"I don't know any of this for sure, of course," Tiger Lily concluded, still stroking the hair of the sleeping Pan.

"I never asked him...and I never will."

She could, however—and now did—ask an odd question of Alice.

"What is an *orphanage*, Alice?"

Though taken somewhat aback by the question, Alice explained to the Indian maiden as best she could the description and the function of such social institutions.

"Why do you ask, Tiger Lily?"

"Because of something the little bird Tinker Bell once told me," Tiger Lily replied. "She'd been drinking quite a bit of fairy nectar at the time, though, so I've never been sure she knew what she was saying."

"And just what did she say?"

"She told me that Peter had once lived in such a place. The way she described it, it was the most horrible place imaginable.

"She claimed it was there that she first laid eyes on Peter. How or why she came to be there she couldn't or wouldn't say.

"But she did say she took an immediate liking to this wretched waif. They were kindred spirits, I suppose." Alice thought she detected a little envy in Tiger Lily's voice.

"It was she who helped him escape from that awful place; she then showed him the way to Neverland.

"Except for those occasional, brief trips back to the Real World…he's never left."

As if he knew what the girls were saying, even in his sleep, Pan began to thrash about on his furry bed. His moans grew louder and a tear squeezed free from beneath tightly shut eyelids.

Tiger Lily hurriedly took hold of him. "Shh-shh-shh," she hushed, gently cradling him in her arms like a baby and rocking him back and forth to comfort and quiet him.

Though she knew she probably shouldn't, Alice felt somewhat uneasy watching this rather intimate, private moment between the maiden and the eternal boy. She decided to leave then and go for a short walk.

She first snatched up a blanket covered with intricate geometrical designs, for protection from the chill of the late night air. Draping it over her head and shoulders and pulling it snugly around her body, she stepped through the door flap of the lodge.

Outside, after walking a short distance that put her just on the outer edge of the village, Alice stopped and inhaled deeply, enjoying the bracing sting of the cold air on her lungs.

As she stared up at the stars, she also thought about her parents and of how much more fortunate than Peter she had been in this regard.

She re-imagined some of the many happy times she had spent with them and found that such pleasant thoughts of them eased the pain of their passing. She was thankful for that.

Gazing up at the beautiful mantle of the night sky also made her think of the far-off place that Pan had called Foreverland. She wondered if such a land really, truly existed—and if she would ever see it.

So captivated was she by the divine mantle of the twinkling, starlit night that Alice saw and heard nothing else—until a slightly smoky smelling hand clamped down over her mouth from behind and she felt herself being dragged off into the nearby forest!

Chapter 30

"*Y*ou grabbed the wrong girl!"

These angry words were shouted by the warrior Little Panther and were directed at the cowering and befuddled Starkey.

The pirate was dumbfounded. "I was *sure* it was Tiger Lily," he practically whined. "With my own eyes, I saw her step out of Man Alone's lodge, wearing an Indian blanket.

"*Every* girl in the village wears an Indian blanket, you idiot," Little Panther snarled, poking the side of Starkey's thick skull with one finger.

"They're all *Indians*!"

They were inside Little Panther's lodge and on the floor of it to one side sat the frightened Alice, her hands tied behind her back as she listened in confusion to this angry harangue.

"Let me explain it to you again, Starkey," Little Panther said to the frightened pirate.

"If we kidnapped Tiger Lily, we could threaten to *kill* her unless her father removed his headdress of leadership and passed it on to *me*." He waved a dismissive hand toward Alice.

"*This* girl means *nothing* to Man Alone! That means she's *worth* nothing—as a hostage or as a negotiating weapon.

"What's *more*—the entire village will now be on the alert to keep an even closer eye on their precious Tiger Lily." He turned to look at two of his followers, who had been standing quietly near the captive Alice.

"Take her out and throw her off the cliff," he said coldly. Without questioning his order, the braves grabbed hold of Alice.

"Hold on, guv'nor!" Starkey suddenly exclaimed, inserting himself between Little Panther and the girl. "Let's not be too hasty!"

"What do you mean?" Little Panther demanded.

"Just this, your lordship. Now that I've had the chance to see the lass up close, I know that she's connected to Peter Pan!" Starkey could tell that had piqued the warrior's interest.

"That's right," Starkey went on. "Pan—the boy you hate so deeply. I saw him and her together when I was spying on the village on your behalf.

"Thick as thieves, they was. Which means she still might be of some use to you, my friend."

"*Pah!*" Little Panther scoffed, turning his back on all the others in the tipi.

Unsure what this gesture signified, they all remained unmoving.

When at last he slowly turned back around to face them, Little Panther had a sly, evil grin twisting his lips.

Something about the way he looked frightened Alice even more than had the prospect of being dashed to death on the rocks!

Chapter 31

The next morning found the entire main Indian village in an uproar. Alice had gone missing in the night and when there was still no sign of her after sunrise, Pan quickly organized a search party to try to locate the girl.

"Look!" someone called out loudly.

A rumbling murmur arose among all the members of the village as the pirate named Starkey approached from the direction of the rebel Indians' small encampment.

As bold as brass, Starkey strutted into the village. He walked right past Pan without acknowledging the boy's presence, and did not stop until he reached a spot just a few feet away from the entrance of Chief Man Alone's rounded lodge.

"Man Alone!" Starkey called out harshly. "Come out and listen, for I have news you will want to hear!"

It was but a moment's passing before the noble old chief pushed through the door flap of his dwelling. His daughter Tiger Lily came with him and stood beside him, just as Pan did when he rushed up a heartbeat later.

"I bring news of the girl with long hair the color of corn," Starkey said, speaking loudly enough to be heard by everyone clustered around him.

"What news?" Pan demanded, then looked apologetically at Man Alone for speaking before the chief could. The old man smiled and patted the boy on the shoulder.

"She is being held by his lordship, Little Panther," Starkey announced, confirming Pan's greatest fear.

"These are his terms," Starkey continued smugly. He pointed straight up with one finger.

"When the sun reaches its highest point today," the pirate said, lowering his hand and pointing at Pan, "the boy who calls himself Peter Pan will come alone to the center of the rock bridge that leads to land's end.

"There, he will be met by Little Panther and the two of them will join in a hand-to-hand battle—to the *death*!"

Fresh murmuring arose among the tribespeople and Starkey grinned with great satisfaction, throwing his chest out like a preening peacock.

"If Pan does *not* accept this challenge to combat," the pirate declared, "if he does not arrive at the designated time and place, then one minute *past* noon –

"The girl Alice will be killed and thrown from the bridge!"

Pan started to impulsively charge Starkey but the wise Man Alone grabbed his arm and restrained him. With his back to the pirate, the chief spoke softly to the boy.

"Little Panther's plan is obvious," Man Alone said. "He has been trying for some time now to convince the people that he would make a better leader than I.

"If he can succeed in killing the mighty Peter Pan, while I stand by helplessly—they may begin to believe he is right!"

"But what choice do I have, O Chief?" Pan asked desperately. "If I don't accept Little Panther's challenge—he'll kill Alice!"

"That's true," Man Alone sadly conceded. "If we tried to storm his camp and take her by force, she would probably be the first one killed." He gazed around the village.

"Nor do I want to put my people in a position where they will have to kill their own brothers—even though those brothers have turned their backs on us and joined Little Panther."

"Then there *is* no choice," Pan said grimly.

"There is one other," Tiger Lily said. The words she spoke next had hardness to them, but she truly did not voice them in an unkind or cold way.

"You could do *nothing*. No one would blame you overly; after all, you've known this girl for less than a week. Some would say you owe her nothing—especially not your life."

"But we've been on an adventure together," Pan protested. "You can't just turn your back on a fellow adventurer."

"There is a chance Little Panther will release her if you refuse his challenge," Tiger Lily countered. "He'd have no further use for her, and killing her would simply show him for the monster he is."

"Being a monster—what does he *usually* do to things that are of no use to him?" Pan replied. "Alice is only here because she chose to help me and to help Tink." He shook his head.

"Now I have to help her."

"Of course you do, Peter—for that is what *you* do," Tiger Lily responded in resignation. Little Panther's reputation as the strongest warrior in the village had been rightly earned and she greatly feared the boy could not possibly be a match for him.

Pan took a step toward Starkey, who—being more than a little craven—took a step back.

"Tell your master I accept his challenge, dog," Pan said in a taunting voice. "Today, at noon…I will meet him on the bridge.

"And only one of us will survive!"

Chapter 32

At the appointed hour, Peter Pan strode alone to the middle point of the narrow land bridge. His long dagger rested in its scabbard; his flintlock pistol was thrust into his belt.

Little Panther, on the other hand, being duplicitous in nature, was *not* alone when he walked out to meet the boy. On one side of him walked the sneering pirate Starkey. On the other side of him was one of his Indian followers—Blue Hawk—who in turn was holding onto their fearful captive.

Alice could see that the entire village had gathered at the mainland end of the natural stone bridge behind Pan, to watch what was about to transpire. They looked slightly different than when first she had laid eyes upon them.

The men were stripped down even more naked, having discarded their leggings in favor of nothing more than breechcloths worn around their middles. Their glistening faces and bodies were now daubed with warpaint of different hues and designs. Each bore arms as well. Tufts of hair hung from their belts, which Alice correctly surmised were *scalps*: grisly trophies from earlier battles.

Man Alone and Tiger Lily stood side-by-side at the villagers' forefront. The old chief was carrying a fine, ash bow in his left hand and wore a quiver full of arrows on his back. Tiger Lily tightly gripped a small but no less lethal tomahawk in both hands.

In similar fashion, the band of rebel Indians that followed Little Panther was clustered at its ends of the land bridge, eager to witness the coming battle.

This, they knew, was bound to be the most epic, long remembered and sung about combat since the day a crazed, wounded bear had charged into the middle of their village.

"That's far enough, boy!" Little Panther bellowed, holding one hand palm out toward Pan.

"Are you all right, Alice?" Pan called to the girl. "Have they hurt you?"

"I wouldn't go so far as to say I'm *fine*, Peter," Alice replied, trying very hard to keep a stiff upper lip and not let her voice tremble. "But I'm mostly unharmed."

"See that she stays that way," Pan said through tight lips. The menace in his voice was unmistakable. "Mostly unharmed" to him translated as "partly harmed;" and the thought of Alice suffering at the hands of these brutes filled him with rage.

"You won't *live* to see what becomes of her," Little Panther rejoined. He then momentarily turned his back to Pan and leaned in toward Blue Hawk's ear.

"Whether I defeat the boy or not," he whispered, "the moment the battle ends—kill the girl!" Blue Hawk nodded in acknowledgment of the order.

Little Panther turned away from Blue Hawk and began to walk toward the waiting Pan. From his beaded belt, the Indian pulled forth a knife and a tomahawk. Pan drew his dagger.

At first the two of them remained several feet apart, circling each other warily. Neither had seen the other in battle before and therefore was unfamiliar with each one's style of fighting.

Suddenly, Little Panther lunged forward with his knife and a collective shout rose from the spectators at both ends of the land bridge.

Pan expertly parried the knife thrust with his own blade, but barely succeeded in ducking beneath a swing of Little Panther's tomahawk that would have cleaved the boy's skull.

He sprang toward the Indian, slamming chests with him and shoving him back several steps. Little Panther swung his knife at Pan's middle, but the boy leaped back nimbly out of its way.

Pan then baffled his opponent by throwing his head back and loudly *laughing*!

"This is *fun!*" he shouted lustily, then pointed his dagger like a finger in Alice's direction. "I hope you don't mind if I don't end it *too* soon!"

Man Alone's villagers roared with approving laughter and Little Panther felt his face burn and his breast fill with killing rage.

He charged forward, and though he was simply flailing blindly with knife and hatchet, the assault was so fierce that Pan was forced to let himself be driven back.

Almost too far back, as he felt the heel of one foot stepping over the edge of the land bridge. Coiling his legs beneath him, he then leaped up and over Little Panther, who barely missed striking him as he did so. Pan somersaulted, landed lightly, then spun to face the Indian.

It soon became evident to all the spectators that this was a most evenly matched contest, and the tide of battle flowed back and forth for quite some time.

As the two combatants collided together and clenched, Pan succeeded in hooking his right heel behind Little Panther's left leg and tripping him. The warrior toppled over, falling heavily to the ground with Pan atop him.

This was all that the treacherous scoundrel Starkey could bear to stand and watch. Fearing that Little Panther was about to go down in defeat, Starkey drew his cutlass and rushed forward, meaning to slay Pan from behind!

The cutthroat came to a jolting halt, though, when a heavy blow struck him. Looking down in shock, he saw what appeared to be a feathered stalk blossoming from his chest. There was barely time for it to register on his clouded mind that this was the quivering shaft of an *arrow* before the life drained out of him and he fell dead to the ground.

As he did, a grim-faced Man Alone—who had fired the lethal arrow—lowered his powerful bow.

At that same instant, Little Panther was able to shove Pan off him, sending the boy rolling to one side. Both combatants quickly scrambled back to their feet; again they circled each other, looking for a chance to strike.

Even the energetic Pan was breathing heavily at this point, so strenuous was their struggle. Still, he lithely skipped back to avoid another swinging slash from Little Panther's knife. Simultaneously, he chopped down with the edge of his left hand, striking his opponent's wrist and forcing him to drop his blade.

Before Little Panther could retrieve it, Pan kicked the fallen knife away. It skittered along across the ground and fell over the edge of the land bridge.

"Not that I wouldn't enjoy killing you," Pan said to the Indian, smiling at him tauntingly, "but we can call this a draw right now if you'd like. All you have to do is release the girl and walk away."

Now it was Little Panther's time to smile. But there was no mirth in his, only murder.

With a loud and fearsome cry, he charged straight at Pan, swinging fiercely right and left with his tomahawk. The boy deflected the blows but was forced to yield ground.

The assault had upset his balance and he felt himself toppling over, his breath whooshing from his lungs as he struck the ground. Sensing victory, Little Panther leaped toward him, tomahawk raise high preparatory to a killing blow.

Quicker than it can be told, Pan managed to rise to one knee and thrust forward with his dagger. He felt a shock go up his arm as the long, sharp blade slid between two of Little Panther's ribs before burying itself in his black heart.

The Indian's mouth dropped open, but he made no sound of pain. His arms lowered and his tomahawk slipped from nerveless fingers. Slowly, he staggered back away from Pan—until he slipped off the edge of the land bridge and disappeared from sight.

Panting heavily from want of breath, too exhausted to feel any elation over his victory, Pan rose unsteadily to his feet.

That's when he heard Alice scream!

Chapter 33

Alice was struggling mightily to pull free, but the warrior called Blue Hawk had his arm around her neck, clutching her tightly against him.

The brave had every intention of following the final command his fallen leader Little Panther had given him. He grabbed the hilt of his knife and began to draw it from its sheath.

With no time for conscious thought or planning, separated from Alice by at least twenty feet Pan dropped his dagger and pulled the flintlock pistol from his belt. In what was nearly a single, seamless move, he drew it, aimed it and fired it.

The struggling Alice felt warm liquid splash against the side of her face. Then the arm around her throat relaxed, loosened and slipped away. As it did, the hand attached to the end of it spasmed, clutching the sleeve of Alice's dress and ripping it.

Gripped by total shock, Alice stared blankly down at the prone body of Blue Hawk. There was a gaping hole in one side of his head; his eyes, though still open, saw nothing.

Then, as the awful realization of what had happened sank it, the dazed girl began to scream hysterically.

The next sensation she felt was of another pair of arms encircling her and she struggled fiercely to pull free from them.

"This is madness!" she shrieked at the top of her lungs. "I don't belong here, I don't belong here, I don't belong here!"

"It's all right, Alice," a soft voice whispered in her ear and at the familiar sound of it, the comforting contact of his arms, Alice grew instantly calm and turned her face to smile at Peter Pan.

He smiled back, but then jerked his head to one side. Alice followed his example and saw that all of Little Panther's followers were now marching toward them.

Pan tried to push Alice behind him, but she would have none of that. Instead, after bending down and scooping up the fallen Blue Hawk's knife, she assumed a defiant stance alongside Pan.

At yet another sound, both children turned to look over their shoulders. From the opposite direction, Chief Man Alone and all his braves (plus Tiger Lily) were also approaching the center of the land bridge.

The two factions halted while still several yards apart—and with Pan and Alice still squarely in the middle.

"There has been enough fighting, enough killing today," Man Alone said in a commanding yet compassionate voice. He directed his next words at the followers of Little Panther.

"Your leader is dead and gone," he reminded them forcefully. "But if you still wish to follow his ways, you are free to do so. All you need do is turn around and return to your lodges." He turned sideways and with a slow, sweeping motion of one arm directed their eyes toward the main village.

"But if you wish to rejoin the rest of us—you will be accepted with open arms. Just lower your weapons and come away with us…and it will be as if you never left. We will have a big feast to welcome you back home."

The rebellious braves looked uncertainly back and forth at each other, saying nothing. Each was debating in his own mind whether he or any of the others was capable of or willing to take up the mantle of Little Panther. For each, the answer was "no."

Finally, one of them shoved his tomahawk back into his belt and began to walk forward, his head held high.

It took but a moment for all the others to follow his example. None of them looked at or spoke to Peter Pan as they passed by him. But each laid a hand on his shoulder in passing, acknowledging the bravery and warrior's skill he had exhibited.

"Stay here for a minute," Pan told Alice after the last of the rebel Indians had passed them on their way back to the principal encampment on the mainland.

Pan walked over to the edge of the land bridge and leaned forward so he could peer down. As he had expected, he saw Little Panther lying still and twisted on the rocks far below. Waves splashed all around the body but it showed no signs of movement or life.

The boy grimaced and shielded his eyes with one hand as a bright beam of light shot out from below and struck him full on in the face. Squinting his eyes tightly, he was at last able to discern the source of the beam.

It was caused by sunlight striking and reflecting off a highly polished stone set in a bone choker Little Panther wore around his throat.

A crashing wave swept over the rocks, causing Little Panther's upper body to slide a few inches to one side. This changed the angle at which the beams from the sun struck the jeweled choker, which in turn changed the path of the light reflecting off it.

A particularly strong beam of reflected sunlight lanced to one side, where it struck an outcropping of the land bridge's face. When it did, Pan's eyes widened in surprise.

"What is it?" Alice called to him. "What is it you're looking at?"

Pan looked excited as he stepped back nearer to her. "Remember the line from the riddle?" he said. "It told us we would find the next riddle at the spot where the black cat falls." Alice shook her head, not sure what he was suggesting.

"Don't you see? Little Panther was the 'black cat.' I'll be right back!"

Turning away from her, Pan ran and dived over the edge of the cliff, much to Alice's dismay. Though somewhat daunted by the height she knew the land bridge to be, she forced herself to lean over the edge and look down.

She heaved a sigh of relief when she plainly saw that Pan was not *falling*—he was *flying* down the side of the cliff!

Pan frowned as he lightly landed on one of the big rocks at the base of the cliff. He was certain this was the spot where Little Panther had been lying just moments ago. Pan could still see slick bloodstains on the stone.

But now Little Panther's body was gone!

Pan knew that the most likely and logical explanation was simply that one of the waves crashing over the rocks had lifted Little Panther's lifeless corpse and carried it out to sea.

Still…

Deciding to spend no more time thinking on it at the moment, Pan went down on one knee at the spot where he thought the body had been lying. Estimating the angle of the last beam of light he had seen coming off Little Panther's necklace, he slowly and carefully scanned the rugged face of the cliff.

It took him a few minutes, but at last he spied what he thought was the spot the reflected sunbeam had illuminated enough to reveal itself to his eyes.

" THE TWO FACTIONS HALTED ... "

It was just a small opening amidst the jutting rocks, not nearly large enough to be a cave and located in such a way as to ordinarily be cut off from the sight of anyone looking down from above.

Pan flew upward until he was floating in place directly in front of the opening. Without hesitation he thrust his hand into it; when he withdrew it he was holding a small wooden chest. Clutching it tightly, he flew up to where Alice awaited him.

Their quest was nearly at an end!

Chapter 34

That night, the Indians staged an even larger feast than they had when Pan and Alice had first arrived; this time they celebrated the reuniting of their village into one. Both food and a sort of mint tea were consumed in copious quantities.

Next came the music and the wild cavorting around the fire. It seemed to Alice that Peter was even more exuberant than usual and in even finer form as a dancer.

The celebration on this night had an added feature once the singing, dancing and music had died down: the telling of stories.

To signal the beginning of this round of entertainment, Chief Man Alone walked into the center of the ring of revelers and raised one arm. In response, most of the noise around him dimmed and died.

"Once," he began, speaking firmly, "in the long ago time, there was a young brave of this village. He was not the biggest of men. He was not the strongest or the fastest or the bravest. He was not the wealthiest." He smiled slyly.

"But luckily—he *was* the *handsomest!*"

All those hanging onto the chief's words burst into raucous laughter.

"It's him!" Tiger Lily whispered, tugging excitedly at Alice's arm. "He's telling a story about himself!"

"And there was a certain young maiden in the village as well," the chief continued. "Tall and fair; so beautiful that the sea and the sky were envious of her. She was called Touched By Sunlight."

"My *mother!*" Tiger Lily said breathlessly, clasping her hands together beneath her chin as she listened raptly.

"As you might expect," Man Alone told his audience, "Touched By Sunlight was much desired by the young braves of the village. But of all of them, she looked with most favor upon the poor, good-looking fellow."

Again, a ripple of laughter.

"Yet it was her father who had final say over who she could wed, and he expected her suitors to woo both her and him with fine gifts.

"One warrior brought a large bundle of fine pelts and laid them at the father's feet. A great hunter and trapper, he had brought the fur of wolves and foxes and even bears.

"A second warrior had carried in a new canoe to give to the father. Made with his own hands, it was strong and sturdy.

"The third warrior presented the father with a new bow made of ash wood, along with a quiver of straight arrows, a new hunting knife and a tomahawk.

"The fourth suitor was the poor brave. It seemed he had brought nothing but himself and stood alone, gazing longingly in silence at Touched By Sunlight.

"'What's this?' the maiden's father said. 'You come empty-handed to woo my daughter? You bring no gift at all?'

"'You're *wrong*,' the poor young brave said. 'I mean to give her the greatest gift of all.'

"'What gift would that be?' her father asked, suspicious of the young man's intentions.

"Before replying, the young brave slowly went down on one knee, his eyes firmly fixed on those of Touched By Sunlight.

"'I give her my *heart*,' was all he said.

"The maiden's father grunted and started to wave him away. What was a mere heart when compared to the gifts the other suitors had brought?

"But then his eyes fell upon the face of his daughter and saw the look of love she cast upon the poor young brave at her feet. The thought arose in him that all the other braves had offered their gifts to *him*; only the poor brave had pledged a gift to *her*.

"And so he gave his blessing to their union—and they were wed."

The crowd burst into appreciative cheers. Alice turned to look at Tiger Lily. Though the girl was smiling, it was with trembling lips; and tears rolled down her cheeks.

"Your mother," Alice said with sudden realization. "She's no longer with you, is she?"

Unable to speak, Tiger Lily merely shook her head slowly. Alice put an arm around her shoulders and pulled her closer, sharing her own sorrow and sense of loss over the deaths of her parents.

Having finished his tale, Man Alone left the inner circle and took a seat beside his daughter. This was a signal for all others who wanted to follow his example and regale the other villagers with their stories.

One by one, individual warriors would walk to the center of the ring of celebrants. Standing near the still crackling bonfire, each would recount for all a tale of some great deed he had performed.

The stories were all very good, often quite exciting. But shortly Alice began to feel there was something just a little *off* about them. She suspected that there was more than a small measure of *exaggeration* to them.

As one example: One warrior claimed to have killed a great fish that was so enormous that he had simply swum into its mouth and gutted it from within!

Yet, to continue the metaphor (if not strain it), his audience seemed to swallow willingly his fish tale hook, line and sinker. They cheered and clapped to show their approval.

As you surely must have expected, eventually Pan walked to the fire and began to tell a tale. The yarn he chose to spin was of the serpents in the cave near Mermaids' Lagoon.

"There I stood," he told his listeners, "alone and unarmed in darkness darker than darkest night!"

("Really?" Alice thought. "What became of your torch, your dagger—and *me*!")

"There were at least a *hundred* of the vipers!"

(Alice: "If it was so dark, how did you know how many there were?" Again, she did not ask this question aloud.)

"Each of the serpents was as big around as an oak tree!" Pan continued unabashedly. "With fangs as long as a man's arm!" He leaped about, striking at the air.

"I fought them with fist and foot—punching and kicking. But one of them managed to latch onto me with his powerful jaws—and swallow me up to *here*!" He made a sort of sawing motion with one hand, signifying his waist—and his rapt audience appropriately "ooohed" and "aaahed."

"Before the great snake could swallow the rest of me," Pan told them, "I grabbed its mouth like this!" He demonstrated, grimacing and acting as if he was exerting great effort to pull his arms apart.

"It took all the strength I had, but finally I pried its mouth open so far that its jaw broke—*crack*!

"Even though it was dead, I still held onto its head. I began to swing its body around and around like a giant whip. I lashed all around—crack, crack, crack!—until I drove all the other serpents back into the even darker corners of the cave.

"Dropping the dead serpent, I quickly snatched up the beautiful mermaid who had been captured by the vipers—and flew her to safety!"

With this, Pan spread his arms and dramatically bowed to show that his tale was at an end. The audience rewarded him with rapturous applause.

"Almost *nothing* you just told these poor people was *true!*" Alice hissed at him as he resumed his seat on the ground beside her. Pan merely smiled back at her.

"There's really not much point in *telling* a story if all you're going to tell is the *truth!*" he pronounced officiously.

"Did you really think that any of the yarns that have been spun here tonight was totally true?"

"Well, *no*. But…"

"That's part of the *game*," he informed her. "Everyone knows the stories aren't completely true—and everyone pretends *not* to know. The secret of good storytelling is to have just *enough* truth in it!"

"Why don't *you* tell us a story, Alice?" Tiger Lily prompted.

"Oh, no," Alice demurred. "I really couldn't."

"Who would like to hear *Alice* tell a story?" Tiger Lily shouted. Everyone in the circle roared their approval. Alice still would have declined, had not Peter and Tiger Lily not lifted her up and literally shoved her out near the bonfire.

She stood there awkwardly for a moment, then curtsied as the cheering died down around her. She looked at Pan and thought he had a particularly smug and cocky look on his boyish face. Very well, then, she thought; I'll give them what they want.

"Tonight," she began.

"Louder!" someone called from the audience.

Alice drew herself up straighter and cleared her throat.

"Tonight, ladies and gentlemen," she said in a loud, clear voice, "for your listening pleasure—I shall tell the story of how *I* saved the mighty Peter Pan from the clutches of a monstrous *Yeti!*"

The audience howled with laughter at the very idea. Alice thought Peter might be embarrassed or even angry at her words, but she saw that he was laughing as loudly as anyone, accepting slaps on the back from some of the warriors nearest him.

Getting fully into the spirit of things, Alice told a tale any Indian would have been proud of. In her telling, the number of Yeti grew from one to ten and she added at least four feet onto its height.

As she had seen Peter and others do before her, Alice did not just *tell* her story—she acted it out. At one point she lowered her voice and slowly walked toward a group of children that was hanging onto her every word by this stage in the narration.

"The mighty Pan did not see the great, hairy beast that was quietly sneaking up behind him," she told them. "Until –

"*Raaar!*" With both arms thrust forward, hands curled like claws, Alice gave her most convincing roar and leaped toward the children.

They all screamed in terror and recoiled (as did some of the adults), then began to laugh (as did some of the adults). Children will do this in an attempt to prove that weren't *really* afraid (as will some adults).

At the climax of the story, just as poor Pan was about to become a snack for the Yeti, Alice—with her bare hands—was able to bring a rockslide crashing down upon their heads and snatch the boy away from its clutches.

As Peter had done before her, Alice then took a bow to hardy and approving cheers from her audience. Returning to her seat, she made a jerking motion with her head toward Peter.

"And *that*, Mister Pan," she said haughtily, "is how you tell a story!"

Chapter 35

The sun had lifted completely above the eastern horizon the following morning as Tiger Lily escorted Pan and Alice to the southern edge of the Indian village.

Alice thought that she looked right splendid in the new wardrobe she now sported. The dress she had worn into Neverland had been so thoroughly soaked, soiled, ripped and torn as to resemble the garb of a distressed and indigent vagrant.

Tiger Lily had been so nice as to offer up one of her own, soft doeskin dresses, which Alice gratefully accepted. After admitting rather enviously that Tiger Lily was a bit more full-figured than was she, Alice had done enough nipping and tucking that it now fit her perfectly.

At the back of her head, a large eagle feather was now laced in her hair and dangled down at a slight angle. The feather was the mark of a warrior, and the villagers all agreed that Alice had earned the right to wear it.

"Are you sure you can't stay just a little longer?" Tiger Lily asked, reaching out and squeezing Pan's left hand.

"I'm afraid we haven't the time," Pan explained with genuine regret. "Tink's about to run out of it."

"Of course," Tiger Lily agreed. "When you get her back—give her my best."

"I will."

"Where are you going next?" the Indian maiden asked.

"We're not sure," Pan replied before Alice could do any more than start to open her mouth. Pan pointed to the small chest in her arms, inside which lay the riddle that would direct them to the final chest: the one containing the treasure Queen Sangramore desired.

"We've decided to put in a few miles before opening it up and reading the riddle that will lead us to our final challenge."

So intently was Tiger Lily gazing at Pan that she failed to notice the odd look on Alice's face, elicited by Pan's last statement.

"Well, good-bye, then," Tiger Lily said sadly. Impulsively, she threw both arms around Pan's neck, hugging him as tightly as she could.

"Don't let anything bad happen to you. And come back to me—to us—soon, Peter. Please."

She pulled away to see Pan smiling confidently. "You shouldn't worry, Tiger Lily." He waved a hand cavalierly. "Whatever lies in store—I'll come through it just fine!"

Alice also smiled—but hers came in response to her silent thought about just how incredibly *dumb* boys could be (though "oblivious" might be a kinder way of putting it).

It was clear to her that poor, childish Peter was totally blind to how strong Tiger Lily's feelings for him were!

The smile lingered on Alice's lips until she and Pan were well out of sight of Tiger Lily and the Indian village. Then it disappeared completely as she spun on her heels to confront the boy angrily.

"Why did you *lie* to Tiger Lily?" she asked of Pan in a harsh, accusatory voice.

"What do you mean?" Pan asked, affecting the mien of the aggrieved.

"You told her we hadn't read the last riddle yet—when you know perfectly well we did so last night, after everyone else had gone to bed!"

Pan hung his head slightly, then lowered himself to take a seat cross-legged on the ground. He patted the sward next to him, indicating he wanted Alice to take a seat also. Rather reluctantly, she did so.

"Open the chest, would you?" he asked softly. "Read the riddle again."

In all the short time she had known him, Alice had never seen Pan look so serious. Still puzzled, she did as he asked.

Go, now, to the darkest place there be,
Where men succumb to violent bent.

For men they were, but now beasts be,
And forbidden hunger is their intent.

Pan sat in silence for quite some time after Alice finished reading, finally shaking his head in grim resolve.

"I don't think there's any mistake," he told Alice. "My first idea about the riddle's meaning is correct."

"Will you share the answer with me?" Alice asked.

"Of course. But I didn't want to tell Tiger Lily; she'd just worry. Or worse—she'd want to come with us."

"I'm not sure *I* want to go there," Alice said, "wherever 'there' is. You make it sound incredibly frightening."

"It is, Alice. More than you can imagine. This last riddle is going to send us to the most mysterious, the most evil and the most dangerous place in all of Neverland."

"More evil than serpents, headless giants and monstrous trees?"

"Much more."

Alice gulped loudly. "What is this place?" she asked and Pan looked at her through eyes narrowed by dire anticipation.

"Cannibal Cove!"

Chapter 36

*P*eter and Alice stood atop a stony ridge, looking down upon what they assumed to be a narrow valley.

They had to assume—because they could not see. All the land below them, for miles around, was blanketed with a fog so thick their eyes could not penetrate its dark folds.

Even where they stood, which was a few miles away, an eerie feeling of dread was pervasive. Apparently, even birds and animals avoided the valley, for no sign of wildlife rose from it. The wind itself seemed not to visit its gloom.

"I've been thinking, Alice," Pan said as he stared down at the enveloping fog bank.

"About what?"

"The time remaining to save Tink is growing short." He drew a deep breath and turned his head to look at her.

"If I don't return from Cannibal Cove within one day of now—I think you should try to make your way back up to the Indian village.

"I'm sure Man Alone and his people will accept you into their tribe."

Alice couldn't believe her ears. "Surely you don't mean to leave me and go down there alone!" she protested.

"I think it would be best," Pan replied.

"Well, I don't! I've been with you every step of the way on this quest of ours, shared every danger equally."

"And you've earned the right to be out of danger for awhile."

She grabbed him by the arm and turned him to fully face her. "Is this about what happened when that Indian nearly killed me and I became hysterical?" Pan said nothing, but his eyes couldn't meet hers.

"All right, I admit it; I lost control for a moment. Can you blame me? I'm not a coward!"

"I know you're not!" Pan was quick to reply. "But a person can only take so much."

At that, Alice put her foot down, literally—stomping the ground. "Now, you listen to me, Mister Peter Pan, Esquire! Anything *you* can take—*I* can take!" She drew herself up even taller.

"We English did not conquer half the known world by being *timid!*"

"Or by being *smart*, apparently!" Pan retorted, thrusting his jaw out and scowling.

"Then I can be just as *dumb* as you are, too!" she declared. "And the longer we stand here arguing, the less time remains for poor Tink!"

Pan glared in silent anger at her, but she didn't flinch. Finally, he threw his arms up in exasperated defeat.

"Fine!" he said.

"Fine!" she replied.

Then the two of them, side-by-side, began the long trek down into the hidden valley.

Even as the two children were beginning their descent, the pirate Captain James Hook was standing on the bow of his ship the *Jolly Roger*. A cooling breeze came off the sea, swirling his long locks and refreshing him. He shuffled his feet to maintain his balance as the ship began to turn.

"We're comin' about, Cap'n," Mister Smee informed Hook, walking forward to stand beside him. "Then we'll set our course for Pirate's Cove."

"Good…good," Hook said absently, but it was clear his mind was in another place, another time.

"Is ever'thin' all right, sir?" Smee asked.

"Fine, sure. Fine." The bo'sun removed his cap, crushing and twisting it in his callused hands.

"Might I be allowed to ask you a question, sir?"

"Yes, yes. What is it?"

"Well, beggin' yer pardon, Cap'n…but it's always seemed to me that you wuz cut from a bit finer piece o' cloth than what you might consider to be your typical buccaneer.

"Might I inquire as to how you came to *be* a pirate?"

Hook smiled thinly; this was the very thing upon which he had been ruminating.

"Would it surprise you to learn, Mister Smee," he told his mate, "that I actually come from a very good family? Their name isn't Hook, of course.

"They are of an old, proud, even somewhat prestigious line. They saw that I was educated at a rather famous public school." His voice took on a colder tone.

"And then they *disowned* me—claiming my misdeeds had brought shame upon the family. That's when I changed my name and took to the seas.

"I found myself to be a very good pirate—if such a word as 'good' can be applied to a buccaneer. By stealth, by strength and by *murder*—I rose through the ranks to command my own ship.

"And she's a good ship, isn't she, Mister Smee?"

"Aye, Cap'n. The finest I've ever sailed or served on!"

"And it was a good life we had aboard her, wasn't it? At least until the Royal Navy chased us into the blasted Sargasso Sea—and we ended up *here*, in Neverland!"

"But that hasn't made her any less fine a ship, sir."

"No, it hasn't, Smee. She's served us well."

"Aye." Smee lowered his voice. "I do have another question, sir."

"Out with it, Mister Smee."

"It's about Her Ladyship—the Queen of Diamonds."

"Go on."

"When this business is all done and we have the treasure in our hands—do you mean to do the queen in?"

"That *would* be the appropriately evil thing to do, wouldn't it?" Hook said. "And probably the smart thing." He sighed deeply.

"But something's happened that I've never experienced before, Smee. I've actually grown *fond* of the woman.

"That being the case…I mean to play fair with her."

"Well and good, Cap'n. But do you think *she* means to play fair with *you*?" Smee asked. Hook's heart sank slightly at the query…for he was unsure of the correct answer.

Indeed, up on the bridge of the ship, Queen Sangramore (with her pet crocodile at her side) stood and watched Captain Hook closely.

"The man *is* a pirate, you know," she said to the reptilian carnivore. "And he no doubt means to betray me once the treasure is in our possession. So it only stands to reason that I should betray *him* first!" She looked down at her pet.

"You'd like it if Mommy gave him to you as a juicy midnight snack, wouldn't you, precious?"

The crocodile growled in gustatory anticipation, as if he had fully understood the question.

"Oh, but just *look* at him, the poor dear," Sangramore said wistfully. "He's quite dashing and even handsome—in that cruel sort of way I so adore." She sighed heavily, even as she stroked the crocodile's scaly head.

"I hate to admit it…but I think I like the man even more than I like *you*!"

Chapter 37

"I think I forgot something," Alice said.

Pan paused and looked back at her. They had stealthily made their way down into the valley and entered the dense fog bank.

"It's too late to go back for it now," he told her.

"It's not a thing," she said.

"Then what is it?"

"In all the excitement of yesterday, I neglected to thank you properly for saving me from that horrible Indian who meant to slit my throat."

"That's what I was there to do," Pan replied.

"Still; I know how precious powder and ball are to you. I am grateful and most honored that you felt me worthy of expending your resources."

"You might not be so eager to thank me once you see what I've let you talk me into allowing you to enter into," Pan said forebodingly.

"Oh, surely this place—gloomy as it is—isn't *literally* peopled by cannibals, is it?" Alice asked (Rather naively, Peter thought, given all she had already encountered in Neverland!).

"There's a reason they don't call this '*Fish Eaters*' Cove'," he replied to her.

"I don't care *what* they call it," Alice persisted. "I still have a hard time believing it—especially given that there are so many *other*, perfectly non-abominable things to eat in Neverland."

"These monsters aren't like that poor, ignorant Yeti," Pan explained.

"They know good and well what lies beyond this valley.

"They *choose* to dine on human flesh!"

"But…but *why*?"

Pan shrugged. "Some say it is because they were placed under a *curse*, centuries ago. Some say they believe that when you consume another man you absorb his strength, courage and knowledge into yourself.

"Some say human flesh is the only food that will sustain their own lives, while others say they are pure evil in human form."

"What do *you* say, Peter?" Alice asked.

"I say they do it—because they *like* to!"

Alice shivered slightly. "Well, in the end I suppose it doesn't really matter why they do it, does it?"

"Just make sure this doesn't become *your* end!" Pan declared.

"One thing that might work in our favor," he went on, "is the fact that there are understandably fairly few of them.

"Knowing precisely who, what and where they are, most human dwellers in Neverland are smart enough to give them, their valley and their cove a wide berth.

"Nor do the cannibals ever roam far from their foggy domain. They shun the light because it places them at a disadvantage in the open.

"They neither make nor carry weapons, even of the most primitive variety. But they have claws and teeth nearly worthy of any predatory animal."

"If you're trying to frighten me, Peter," Alice said in hushed tones, "you're doing an admirable job of it!"

"Now you know why I tried to convince you to stay behind, Alice," Pan said.

"And I appreciate that," she replied. "I really do. But in for a penny, in for a pound, as those who know about such things say."

"What does that mean?"

"It means lead on, Peter—and I'll be right behind you!"

Pan placed a finger to his lips and Alice nodded. The valley through which they walked was heavy with foliage, so they stepped softly and carefully to avoid making unnecessary noise.

Yet sounds there still were: faint rustlings in the underbrush from time to time. Alice devoutly hoped that the noises indicated there were still a few small animals that made this place their home and not that the noise meant cannibals were watching and following them.

The very idea filled Alice with dread. Maybe going to live with Elsbeth and Aubrey and eventually marrying some stuffy older gentleman wouldn't be *such* a bad thing, she found herself thinking. At least she would never have to worry about the possibility of becoming someone's *porridge*!

But neither was she likely to have many true *adventures* in such a life, either. She was rather surprised to find that she thought she much preferred being *here.*

Pan stopped a step ahead of her, cocking his head to one side and cupping his hand around his ear. Alice followed his example.

They were both able to make out a low sound, almost like that of chanting that was coming from a faraway cathedral. Not knowing what else to do, the two children cautiously followed the sound.

Not long afterward, they found themselves kneeling at the spot where the forest around them ended. Ahead of them was a small clearing, butting up against a watery cove.

Alice spied what appeared to be a few huts, though they were of the simplest, crudest and most primitive nature: little more than a few palm fronds laid diagonally across a bare, rickety wooden frame. A lean-to, she believed such habitats were called.

Her eyes slid from them to the center of the clearing—and her hand clamped over her mouth to stifle a gasp that might have given away their location.

She had just gotten her first good look at *cannibals*!

Chapter 38

They were about a dozen in number, simply standing together in a rough circle. It was from their blackened and cracked lips that the sound as of chanting emanated.

"Whatever are they doing?" Alice asked in a whisper.

"Saying *grace*, perhaps?" Pan quipped.

"That's not funny!" Alice hissed, punching Peter in the arm (His good arm, not the one that still bore a wound).

The cannibals seemed to be even more naked than had been the Indians, with nothing but thin, tattered and filthy strips of cloth tied around waists that were not as big around as was Alice's.

Their skin was a pallid gray color. Their pates were partially bald, with patches of oily hair that were thin, long and scraggly. Their eyes bulged grotesquely from sunken sockets.

Each and every one was horribly thin; the bones of their ribs and pelvises showed clearly through the skin.

"They look as though they haven't eaten in weeks," Alice observed.

"It's possible they haven't," Pan replied. "As I said, with time it has become increasingly difficult for them to find unwitting prey of the species they prefer."

"That being the case," Alice said most logically, "do they resort to dining on each other?"

"Oh, no," Peter replied. "Even cannibals have *some* ethics, after all."

"Which is more than some politicians can honestly claim, as my father often said," Alice commented.

"A person could almost feel sorry for the poor, gaunt buggers," Pan declared. "You know—if they weren't trying to eat you!"

"Yes, well—let's feel sorry for them *after* we're out of this dreadful place, shall we?" Alice replied.

"Agreed."

The cannibals in the circle had been standing around what appeared to be no more than the dead stump of some long-since fallen tree. As the two children continued to watch them from hiding, they began a sort of shuffling, sideways dance around the stump. Their mumbled chanting grew ever louder.

There was now even musical accompaniment of a sort to their ritual. Off to one side, a cannibal methodically banged a stick against a hollowed log while another blew on a short, hollow reed that seemed capable of producing only one monotonous tone.

From one of their nearby, pitiful hovels a pair of fellow cannibals emerged, carrying a short litter between them. Resting atop the litter was a small *chest*—virtually identical to all the others Alice and Pan had retrieved over the course of their quest!

One difference was that this box appeared to be a bit more ornate: several large gems were embedded in its sides and lid.

The litter bearers lowered their load, then picked up the chest and reverently set it atop the lowly tree stump. From a nearby pile, they gathered bits of kindling, laying it on the ground around the stump before joining their fellow cannibals.

From the largest and sturdiest of the lean-tos, a final member of the tribe emerged, carrying a sputtering torch. His face was decorated with stripes of white paint and Alice was sickened to see that, atop his head, he wore the upper portion of a human *skull* as if it were a hat!

This cannibal began to chant a sing-song incantation in cannibalese whilst making arcane motions in the air with his torch. Alice assumed he was a priest of some sort --of what kind of ungodly religion, she couldn't imagine.

The priest finally walked all the way around the tree stump, lighting the kindling as he did so.

As the flames rose higher, the illumination given off by them began to strike the gems adorning the chest and reflect back as lances of multicolored light. This light playing across their countenances seemed to plunge the worshipful cannibals into an almost ecstatic state.

They appeared to revere the chest as some sort of heavenly artifact. The steps of their "dance" quickened and their guttural chanting grew louder.

"I don't see any *lady* cannibals," Alice quietly observed.

"You won't," Pan declared. "Because no lady would ever take up such disgusting dining habits!"

"Ahh," said Alice. "You're quite right!" Her face then scrunched in concentration.

"But now that we seem to have found the final chest," she inquired, "how do we go about snatching it?"

Pan grinned almost mischievously. "In this particular case, Alice—I think the direct approach is called for!"

Chapter 39

A short time later, the cannibals were continuing to work themselves into a sort of muted frenzy. What the purpose of this ritual was, one can only imagine. Perhaps even such nearly mindless ghouls as this had some sense of a power higher than themselves and used this to commune with it.

Or perhaps cannibals simply like to dance!

Whatever its purpose, the ritual came to a crashing halt when a shrill whistle split the air and intruded upon their music, their chanting and their dancing. As one they turned to see the source of the whistling.

Just outside the cover of the forest, on the northern edge of the clearing, Peter Pan stood in full view. His legs were spread, his fists rested on his hips—and he laughed heartily at the cannibals' confusion.

"Take a good look, snaggle-tooths!" he shouted at them, spreading his arms out to his sides and pirouetting lightly.

" ...THEY GATHERED BITS OF KINDLING ... "

"Supper is served!"

The boy then turned and bounded nimbly back into the concealing foliage of the thick forest.

With a concerted, rusty sounding scream, the cannibals all rushed off in pursuit of this tasty-looking morsel, leaving their small village empty and unattended.

A few minutes later, as sure as she could reasonably be that not a single cannibal remained behind, Alice stepped from her place of hiding in the forest on the south side of the clearing. Careful but determined, she strode toward the stump upon which sat the chest.

By this time, the fire encircling the stump in the center of the cannibal village had begun to die down naturally. It was therefore no trouble at all for Alice to hop over it, walk over to the stump and grab the gem-encrusted chest that rested atop it.

She devoutly wished that Peter were having just as easy a time.

For his part, Pan felt little concern about keeping ahead of his pursuers. Being in a constant state of half-starvation, cannibals tended not to be so fast or agile as most other predatory animals.

Their obsessive predilection for human flesh utterly baffled the boy. He'd met quite a few people in his life—some of them very nice—but he could not honestly imagine any one of them that would have tasted nearly as delicious as a nice, fat, fried chicken!

Such thoughts were secondary at the moment to staying out of the clutches of those hunting him. He didn't want to get *too* far ahead of them, though—lest they give up the chase and return to their village before Alice had time to carry out her part of the plan.

Pan made no effort to keep quiet as he passed through the forest foliage; in fact, he made sure to produce as much noise as possible so he would be easy to follow. From time to time he would stop and listen to make sure he was still being pursued.

Still, the ponderous predators lost track of him at one point and began to mill about, grunting in perplexity at each other.

"*Yaaa!*" came a shout from above.

Pan came swinging on a vine from out of a tree, his trajectory carrying him right through the midst of the cannibals and sending several of them sprawling like bowling pins.

"You're going to have to do a lot more than just *sing* for you supper!" he taunted them.

He waited until they were all back on their feet, then leaped down off his tree perch and again sprinted away through the forest, loudly laughing as he went.

Any time he feared he was getting so far ahead of the cannibals that they might give up the chase, he would stop until they were within sight. He would then mock them by flapping his arms like wings and cawing like a crow before resuming running.

At last, though, Pan figured Alice must surely have had plenty of time to have grabbed the chest and made her way a safe distance away from the cannibal conclave. He stopped his running, bending over to place his hands on his knees while he slowly sucked in lungfuls of air. The merry chase had left him winded but cheerful—so much so that he again threw his head back and started to laugh.

But the laughter stopped when two pairs of desiccated gray hands suddenly grabbed him from behind!

Chapter 40

With the final chest in her possession, Alice left the cannibal village and headed due south away from it as rapidly as the thick foliage and the vision-obscuring fog would allow.

Pan, before they split up, had instructed her to keep going and not stop until she had left the perpetual fog bank well behind her. This would signify that she was clear of the cannibals' normal hunting grounds. Once this was accomplished, she was to wait for Pan to find and rejoin her.

Even after ascending to a level above the fog, Alice kept climbing until she had crossed over the top of the hills surrounding the valley. Once on the downside she picked a spot that gave her sufficient protection from detection while still affording her a clear field of vision back the way she had come. Here, she decided to wait for her companion.

With each passing minute that she waited, though, Alice became more and more concerned that the cannibals might have captured Peter.

Finally, she made the decision to count to one thousand. If Pan hadn't shown up by the time she finished her count, she was determined to ignore his instructions about leaving him behind.

She had no intention of going on in any direction without him; she would instead head straightaway back to the cannibal village and save him from becoming the main course at some unholy feast!

As her silent count reached number 732, she began to feel more certain that Pan had indeed fallen into enemy hands.

"*Aaaa!*" she shrieked as something suddenly dropped straight down out of the sky, landing practically at her feet and sending a shower of dead leaves flying up and about in all directions!

His distinctive laughter told her before her eyes did that its was Pan himself now standing before her, affecting his most cocky stance. In the instant, the girl's fear, concern and anxiety for him turned into the single emotion of anger.

Much to Pan's surprise, she hauled off and hit him with a good, old-fashioned roundhouse right-hand punch that knocked him flat on his bottom!

As sometimes happens to ladies, especially young and proper ones like Alice, her anger immediately vanished as she saw the sprawled Pan shaking his head in a daze.

She dropped to her knees beside him, cupping his head in her hands and stroking his hair. "Oh, I'm sorry, Peter," she said most sincerely. "Are you all right?"

To her relief, Pan laughed. "If I haven't told you before, Alice, you throw quite a punch—for a *girl!*" He wiggled his sore jaw back and forth gingerly. "I may succeed in turning you back into a child after all!"

"Oooh!" Alice huffed. "Ouch!" Pan exclaimed as she released his head and it banged back down on the ground. She then plopped fully down on the grass beside him, folding her arms over her bosom and scowling.

"Sometimes I think the whole *purpose* of boys is simply to aggravate girls!" she declared.

Lifting himself to a sitting position, Pan laughed again before turning the tiniest bit more serious.

"Did you get the treasure chest?" he asked Alice.

"I did," she replied, lifting it up and handing it to him. "Did you have any trouble getting away from the cannibals?"

"Pfff! Not at all!" he said breezily. "Being half-starved, they can't run very fast—and being more than half *stupid*, they can't think very fast either. It was easy to lose them!"

As has been established in regard to Peter, this was one of those occasions when what he told Alice was a bit of a lie—or "make believe" as he would have preferred to call it. Or maybe (just maybe) he simply did not want her to know how close he had come to death.

For two of the cannibals (doubtless better fed than their brethren), knowing the forest ways better than Pan did, had succeeded in heading him off and laying hands on him.

Their plan, if it can be called that, was simple (for their malnourished minds were capable of nothing more): to engage the boy in struggling with them long enough for the rest of his pursuers to catch up, join them and overpower their prey by weight of numbers.

The pair succeeded in pulling Pan off his feet and dragging him to the forest floor. Though they outnumbered him two-to-one, the combined weight of their cadaverous bodies was not much more than his own, so they had to struggle mightily.

So closely were they locked in combat that Pan could feel their collective breaths wash over him; he nearly gagged from the smell of death, decay and desperation that they exuded.

He thrashed about with arms and legs; he managed to punch one and dust flew from it as if it were an old rug being beaten. Pan twisted back and forth to avoid the cracked, filthy fingernails with which they sought to claw him. Their jagged, rotted teeth clacked as they snapped at him.

Finally, in the midst of the struggle, Pan was able to lay his hand upon the hilt of his dagger. Pulling it from his scabbard, he plunged it into the side of one of his attackers.

Issuing a shrill, animal-like wail of pain, the cannibal lurched back and slammed against the trunk of a tree. Looking down at the wound, he saw the brackish green slime that passed for blood in the veins of a cannibal. It was neither gushing nor truly flowing from the wound; but was more oozing like thick sap from a tapped tree.

The smell of escaping blood (or whatever you might choose to call this bizarre fluid) caused the other cannibal to pause and sniff hungrily at the air. Ethics or not, the smell was tempting to him.

A moment later, he got the chance to smell his own life liquid. Distracted as he was, the cannibal was an easy target for Pan's flashing blade and the dagger plunged deeply into the monstrosity's sunken chest. He toppled limply to one side.

Wanting no trace of cannibal blood to desecrate his cherished dagger, Pan wiped the blade thoroughly clean on the grass before returning the weapon to its sheath. He then turned his back on his dead and dying attackers and leaped into the underbrush. From that point he had no further trouble.

Whether he fibbed to Alice in his account primarily to spare her from knowing just how much peril he encountered or just to make it seem like his escape from the cannibals had been easier and more skillful than it actually was, even he probably didn't know for sure. Or care.

"Let's have a closer look at the prize we've worked so hard to obtain," he said, examining the final chest.

"It doesn't look much different than all the other ones we've found along the way," he said with obvious disappointment.

"There's one way in which it is *quite* different," Alice countered. She pointed to one of the gems embedded in it.

"That's why it sparkled so in the firelight," she said. "The other chests were relatively plain wooden boxes. This one is covered in what appear to be precious *jewels*. There must be a small fortune here in those alone!"

"Then, think of what must be *inside* the chest," Pan said. "A huge diamond, perhaps. Or a giant pearl or emerald."

"Shall we open it and find out?" Alice asked excitedly.

"Here's *another* way this chest is different," Pan replied, showing her that the lid of this box was held closed by a small but heavy padlock.

"Besides," he continued, "we don't have much time left if we're going to make it to Pirates Cove before Captain Hook and the Queen of Diamonds do something terrible to Tink!"

"Oh, my, yes!" Alice exclaimed in dismay. "I'd almost forgotten. Heaven only knows what horrible things they've already been doing to her!"

Chapter 41

"I'll grill your bloody wings in butter and eat them for my supper, you foul fairy!" Captain Hook bellowed.

In response, Tinker Bell giggled with gusto.

In an effort to cut through the tedium of the past week, Hook had made the mistake of teaching Tink how to play *chess*.

Alas for him, she had proven to be an eager and adept pupil—and had mastered the complex game so quickly and so thoroughly that she had just beaten the pirate two matches in a row!

"Admit it," he snarled. "You've been *cheating*!"

"How could I cheat?" Tink protested. "I'm in a *cage*!"

(This was true. Hook was too smart and far too suspicious by nature to allow her out of her tiny prison. She had been compelled to call out her chess moves and have the pirate physically make them for her.)

"Be that as it may," Hook argued, "there's something *wrong* here!"

"Orrrrr," Tink countered, holding up one finger. "Is it possible that you are such a marvelous instructor that you have passed every bit of your knowledge and skill on to me in record time?"

"Eh?" Hook had not considered this possibility and Tink could tell by the expression on his face that the notion flattered him. Still, she thought it would probably be wise to deliberately *lose* the next match.

Mister Smee came bursting into the captain's cabin at that moment. "The queen says it's time!" he blurted breathlessly.

"Ah-ha!" Hook exulted. He snatched up the small birdcage holding Tink off its place atop the table where the chessboard rested. With Smee close behind, he raced from the cabin.

The two pirates brought the captive fairy out onto the main deck of the *Jolly Roger* before Smee split away to go attend to his other duties. The Queen of Diamonds was already there, impatiently tapping one foot against the deck's planking. As always, her devoted crocodile was right beside her; he was even tapping one clawed foot in time with hers.

"Where *is* he?" she snapped. "Where is that infernal boy with my treasure?"

"Peter will be here," Tink fiercely asserted.

"For *your* sake, bug—he'd better be!" Sangramore screeched, grabbing the sides of the birdcage and sending Tink tumbling back to fearfully cringe against its restraining bars.

"They're all there, all right," Peter Pan said. From a safe distance away, he was watching the activity aboard the *Jolly Roger* through the lens of one of Captain Hook's own spyglasses, which Pan had purloined on one of his salvage trips to the ship in the months after Hook had disappeared and been presumed dead.

Pan and Alice were safely hidden on a hilltop just north and slightly east of the cove where the *Jolly Roger* was now anchored once again, its stern turned toward them.

Pan smiled as he lowered the spyglass. "That wicked, wicked woman who calls herself a queen chose me to do her dirty work for her because she thinks I'm clever." He forcefully collapsed the spyglass down to its normal length with a loud clack.

"And I'm about to show her just *how* clever!"

Pan looked questioningly at Alice. "Are you ready, Alice? Do you know what you have to do?"

Alice, clutching the final chest, nodded but looked pensive even as she handed the box over to Pan.

"But what happens when this is all over, Peter?" she asked tentatively. "What will you do then?"

Pan gave a nonchalant shrug. "I'm sure the first thing we'll do is hold a big celebration with all the fairy folk.

"After that…who knows? Maybe I'll finally try to go find Foreverland!"

Alice smiled wanly. Though she had directed her question at her companion—it really applied more to her. What would happen to *her* after this adventure came to an end?

(And, as brave people are wont to do, she would not allow herself to even consider the possibility that it could end in failure, even death for her or Peter or both!)

Would she lie down to sleep and wake up to find herself safely back in her London home, in her own bed—convinced that like her adventures in Wonderland this too had been nothing more than a vivid and elaborate dream?

Would there be nothing more left for her to do than live with the reality of losing that home, moving in with her sister Elsbeth and resigning herself to a boring life wed to some perfectly proper but equally boring gentleman?

And why did thoughts of either prospect now fill her with even more dismay and dread than they had before?

Acting on an impulse she would never even have had a few days ago, Alice threw her arms around Pan's neck, pulled him close and kissed him full on the lips!

"Please be careful, Peter," she said, suddenly embarrassed and feeling not at all proper. Her eyes downcast, she stepped back away from the boy, clumsily clasping her hands behind her back.

Pan put one hand under her chin, lifting her face to his. He gave her a sly wink, started to turn away, and then started giggling softly.

"What?" Alice asked, afraid he was being derisive of her.

"This," Peter said, placing his fingers to his lips.

"There was a time when I called kisses 'thimbles.' Can you believe that? Now I know better." Suddenly, a scowl darkened his pretty face.

"I hope that doesn't mean I'm growing up!"

Chapter 42

"Ahoy the ship!"

Captain Hook and Queen Sangramore looked up from the deck of the *Jolly Roger* to see Peter Pan hovering upright in the air some twenty feet above the ship. In the crook of one arm he held the final treasure chest.

"Permission to come aboard?" Pan shouted down.

"Permission—" Hook and the queen shouted back at the same time, then looked somewhat angrily at each other.

Feeling magnanimous (and wanting to get on with it!), the Queen of Diamonds nodded to Hook and gave him a slight wave of her hand.

"Permission to come aboard granted!" Hook called up to Pan.

The boy slowly made his descent, keeping a sharp eye out for any pirate who might be thinking of shooting him from hiding. There being barely enough onboard to be considered a skeleton crew, Smee and the handful of others were too occupied with their duties aboard ship to pay any mind to the hostage transfer about to transpire.

When he finally planted his feet on the ship's deck it was several yards away from where Hook and Sangramore stood with their backs to the doorway leading into the *Jolly Roger's* powder magazine.

"Is that the prize I demanded?" the queen asked, pointing toward the box in Pan's hands.

"If it wasn't, I wouldn't be here."

"I hope you had a sufficiently difficult time obtaining it," Hook sneered.

"Not at all," Pan replied with a cocky grin. "It was easier than falling off a log—or escaping a hungry crocodile!"

The pirate hissed in anger, raised his hook and started to rush forward, only to be stopped by the hand of the queen.

"Later, darling," she said softly. "*After* we have the treasure." Hook grumbled beneath his breath but stood his ground.

"How do you suggest we do this?" Pan called to them.

"It's simple enough," Queen Sangramore said. "You toss us the chest—and I'll open the cage and release the annoying little bug!"

"*Grrr!*" Tink raged, helplessly shaking the bars of her little prison.

"Nooo," Pan replied, shaking his head. "I don't think that plan works for me."

"Why not?" the queen demanded.

"Because once you've got the box—I don't think I could trust you to keep your word and let Tink go!"

Hook and Sangramore exchanged glances.

"He *does* have a point," the pirate admitted, shrugging. The queen nodded in agreement.

"So what do *you* suggest we do, boy?" she asked Pan. This was just the reply he'd wanted.

"How's this?" Pan said. "You set her cage down on the deck, right there. I'll set the box down right here where I am.

"We then walk toward each other, empty-handed, till we cross paths and reach what we each want."

He stood patiently then as the queen and the captain put their villainous heads together. They discussed things thoroughly in whispers, occasionally casting a suspicious glance at Pan.

"Very well," Sangramore said at last. "Your plan is acceptable to us."

She gracefully lowered herself down—then roughly dropped the bird-cage the rest of the way to the deck.

"*Oww!*" Tink yelped as she was thrown off her feet.

Pan's eyes narrowed angrily at the sight of this deliberate and unneces-sary act of cruelty, but then he smiled. Holding the small treasure chest out in front of him at chest level, he pulled his hands apart so that it too fell to the deck with a clank.

"You'd best hope you haven't damaged my treasure, boy!" Sangramore hissed at him.

"And you'd best hope you haven't damaged my fairy—*woman!*" Pan replied with cold intent.

For long seconds he and Sangramore then engaged in a silent but threat-ening staring contest.

"Oh, let's just get on with it!" Hook finally said with unconcealed impatience.

He strode forward, followed quickly by Sangramore and her crocodile; Pan did the same from his side. The two parties gave each other a wide berth as they passed and continued on toward their respective objectives, making no attempt at treachery.

Unable to fully contain her eagerness, however, the Queen of Diamonds ran the last few steps to the chest, eagerly snatching it up in her hands.

As she gazed at it, she had no idea that all of the jewels that had decorated the outside of the chest were now missing (Pan having plucked them out with the point of his dagger earlier. After all, one never knows when one can use a few precious gems!).

Nor would Queen Sangramore have cared overmuch if she had known this fact; it was what was *inside* the box that held her interest!

She looked to Hook, only to find that his gaze was fixed upon her croco-dile, who in turn was eyeing the pirate with far too much anticipation for Hook's comfort.

Pan ignored them for the moment, bending down on one knee to see for himself whether Tinker Bell was truly unharmed. She smiled up at him and he smiled back, yet he made no effort to release her from the birdcage.

Instead, he put a finger to his lips, signaling for her to remain still.

He then rose, turned his back to the fairy and tip-toed back the way he had come until he was standing right behind the unsuspecting Hook and Sangramore.

The Queen of Diamonds had picked up the chest and was impatiently trying in vain to pull loose the padlock that sealed the lid shut.

"Open it for me, James!" she entreated, shoving the box into Hook's arms.

After eyeing it closely, Hook set the chest back down on the deck and knelt beside it. After working his prosthetic hook into the bowed piece of the padlock, he then slammed his left fist sharply down on the hook. The blow and the leverage combined to pop the lock open.

As Hook tossed the now useless padlock overboard, Queen Sangramore knelt down beside him and anxiously clawed at the lid of the box. Imagine her surprise and dismay when she flung open the chest—only to discover nothing inside but a rolled piece of parchment.

"Not another *riddle*!" the queen moaned.

"Open it up," Hook urged her. "Maybe it's a *map*—showing us the way to the treasure!"

"Yes, of course," Sangramore replied. "That *must* be it!"

Her hands trembling slightly, she pulled the scroll from its resting place and carefully unfurled it.

To her horror—all that was revealed was a blank page!

Sangramore held the parchment up to the sun, hoping its light would reveal an image, but it did not. She turned the page over; she turned it upside down; she turned it sideways and diagonally and left and right.

Nothing.

"This must be some sort of *trick*!" she screeched angrily.

"Or perhaps you're just not looking at it right," a playful voice said from right close behind Sangramore and Hook.

Their heads spun around to see Peter Pan leaning over their shoulders. So startled were they that each fell over onto the deck. Pan, for his part, hopped back a few paces and stood with his hands on his hips, laughing mockingly at them as they lay sprawled before him, their limbs all atangled.

"The blasted boy must have taken the treasure for himself!" Queen Sangramore shouted, pointing an accusing finger at Pan.

"Get him!"

As she and Hook staggered to their feet, Pan turned and bounded across the deck, passing through the door that led into the ship's powder magazine and slamming it shut behind him.

Hook, Sangramore and her crocodile all followed in pursuit of the boy.

So focused were they on him that none of them took note of the fact that the birdcage holding Tinker Bell captive was now nowhere in sight (Nor had Pan scooped it up on his way to the powder magazine). As they expected, when they reached the magazine they found the door had been locked from the inside.

"*Yaaah!*" Captain Hook roared, rearing back and then ramming his hook into the wood of the door. Fiercely he began hacking and slashing at the paneling. It took much effort and repeated strokes of the hook but at last he was able to hack a hole in the door sufficiently large for him to insert his real hand in and unfasten the portal.

He, Sangramore and the crocodile then cautiously entered the somewhat darkened interior of the storage room wherein was kept kegs of gunpowder and boxes of lead balls. They were suspicious of a trap, but they saw no one in the room save themselves.

"The window!" Queen Sangramore exclaimed, pointing toward the square porthole at the rear of the room.

It was hanging wide open!

She and Hook raced to the porthole and looked out. Some distance away, they could see Peter Pan flying away toward the mainland.

And he was not alone.

Dangling beneath him was the girl Alice. Pan was carrying her with his hands under her arms—while in her own hands was cradled the birdcage holding Tinker Bell.

Just as the queen had said earlier, Pan *was* a clever boy. And he had devised a clever plan.

Before meeting with Sangramore and Hook, Pan had taken Alice out to the *Jolly Roger*, flying low over the water of Pirates Cove so as not to be seen by anyone aboard the ship.

Using the tip of his dagger's blade to unlatch it, he had opened the porthole leading into the powder magazine. Leaving Alice hidden inside, he had then flown around to approach the ship from a different direction and began the negotiations for Tink's safe return.

(Pan knew that the pirate Hook and the treacherous Queen of Diamonds would not hesitate to cheat if they got the chance, so it didn't bother him in the least to do a little "cheating" himself!)

Meanwhile, Alice used part of her time inside the magazine wisely, grabbing horns of gunpowder and sacks of lead balls that now hung by straps from her shoulders. (As we will soon see, she had reason to be quite certain that Pan would have need of these extra supplies!)

At the appropriate time, when Hook and the queen had all their attention focused on the chest and its contents and Pan was behind them further blocking their view, Alice had quietly slipped out of the magazine room.

As Tink, smiling gleefully, watched her, Alice picked up the birdcage and just as quietly spirited it away. She retreated back to the darkness of the powder magazine with Tink to await for Pan to join them.

And as the villains of this piece were about to discover, there was yet *another* clever thing Peter and Alice had done before leaping out the porthole and flying away from the ship.

"A *boy*!" Queen Sangramore now railed. "Nothing but a *boy*—and yet he tricked me!" She clenched her fists so tightly that her nails nearly drew blood from the palms of her hands.

"I want him captured!" she screeched. "Yes—and the mewling little girl, too!" Her rage exceeded all bounds.

"I'll boil them in oil! I'll bake them in cookies! I'll—"

"Be *quiet*!" Hook snapped, and Sangramore's breath sucked in loudly.

"How...*dare* you!" she snapped back at the pirate indignantly.

"I mean *listen*!" Hook said, holding up one hand.

Though still feeling angry and insulted, the queen did as he bade. At first, however, she heard nothing but the gentle lapping of the waves against the hull of the pirate ship.

But then she detected a persistent, insistent hissing sound.

"Did that insufferable brat leave a *snake* in here?" she demanded.

"I don't think so," Hook replied, moving carefully about the cabin trying to find the source of the sound.

When he succeeded in doing so, he let out a loud gasp. The queen and the crocodile pressed in close behind him to look.

Too late, they realized that Pan had left behind a most unpleasant "gift" for them when he flew away from the ship.

The hissing sound was coming from a short length of cannon fuse that Pan had lit before diving out the stern porthole with Alice and Tink.

And this rapidly burning fuse ran right into the top of an open cask of gunpowder!

"No," said Hook.

"No," said Queen Sangramore.

(Naturally enough, the crocodile said nothing.)

With two screams and a roar, the three co-conspirators turned to run away, practically falling over each other as they did.

The spark from the burning fuse leaped into the gunpowder, igniting it and causing the entire keg to explode. This in turn caused the keg of powder closest to it to explode—and so on and so on, like falling dominoes.

Multiple explosions, each seemingly louder and more powerful than the one before, tore through the *Jolly Roger*, practically lifting her up out of the water. Flames swept the decks and gaping holes were torn in the hull, allowing torrents of water to rush in.

It was but a matter of minutes before the once-proud *Jolly Roger* was turned into nothing more than a shattered husk that rapidly took on water and sank to the sandy bottom of the cove.

And so ended the largely wasted lives of the pirate Captain James Hook and Sangramore, the beautiful but malevolent Queen of Diamonds.

Probably.

Chapter 43

The first thing Peter and Alice did after witnessing the sinking of the *Jolly Roger* was extricate Tinker Bell from her imprisonment. Bars that were impossible for a tiny fairy to break bent easily under the weight of Pan's dagger used as a pry to push them apart.

"*Yippee!*" Tink shouted ecstatically, zooming out of the cage and flying about in circles that left sparkling trails of fairy dust in their wake.

Just as Pan had predicted, his defeat of the evil pirate and the equally evil queen and his rescue of Tinker Bell were indeed a cause for great celebration upon their subsequent return to the Fairy Forest.

It took a few days' planning, but the bacchanal that resulted was well worth it (and itself went on for more than a full day!). There was much singing and dancing, well into the night. Sweets of all sorts were in plentiful supply and many, many thimbles of fairy nectar were consumed.

(Having learned her lesson from her first encounter with this honeyed ale, Alice made sure to pace herself carefully, downing the drink only one thimble at a time and waiting an appropriate length of time before having another!)

Alice could still only understand small dribs and drabs of the tinkling sound that passed for normal fairy language, but it was enough for her to get the gist of their songs. And of course one doesn't need to understand music to dance to its rhythms.

At what may or may not have been the height of the celebration (It was hard to say with fairy folk; they seemed to have an almost endless capacity for partying!), Alice realized that Pan and Tinker Bell were nowhere to be seen.

Curious, she set out through the trees in an easterly direction. She knew the seacoast lay not far in that direction and thought the two of them might have gone there to gaze at the stars and privately celebrate their reunion. ("Privately" would seem to indicate that *she* was not wanted there, but for once Alice chose to forego decorum.)

"It *is* a lovely night, isn't it?" a rather beguiling voice said from above Alice, giving her a bit of a start.

She relaxed at once when she looked up to see a familiar, toothy grin floating in the air above a nearby tree branch.

"Have you come back for a visit, *Cheshire Cat*?" Alice asked, smiling as, sure enough, the rest of the large, tawny feline appeared around its mouth.

"What can I say? I like music!"

"Have you been enjoying your time here in Neverland?" Alice asked politely.

He flicked his fluffy tail back and forth a few times before answering. "In a manner of speaking I have, I suppose. This can be a rather *dangerous* place, though, can it not?"

"Yes, I suppose that's true."

"And have you ever *seen* so many things constantly trying to *eat* so many *other* things?" he commented.

"Perhaps someone should open a *restaurant* here!" His smile widened as he gazed down at the girl.

"And what about *you*, Alice? Have you enjoyed your time here?"

Alice felt it prudent to give that question a bit of thought before she answered it.

"Well, as you said, Cheshire, it *can* be a very dangerous place. And the people who live here pay far too little attention to what's proper and what's not.

"But I've met some who are truly amazing. Fairies and mermaids. A real, live Indian princess. Mister Yeti. Doctor Philogenias and Footloose." She inhaled deeply.

"Along the way, I've learned that you don't have to be a grown-up to be grown up; and that some grown-ups aren't very grown up at all."

"It sounds like you've learned quite a lot," Cheshire Cat observed.

"You know…I think I have!"

"Then I suppose I should leave you to your lessons," the feline said, and Alice saw him begin to fade away.

"Please don't leave on my account, Cheshire!" she said. "I hope you know

I always welcome your visits!"

"I do know that, Alice," he purred, even as his voice too began to grow dim. "And that makes an old cat feel good!" Only his smile now remained in sight.

"I'll be back. Until then—farewell, Alice. Fare...well."

Then he was gone.

Left alone again, Alice found her eyes drawn to a small point of light flickering in the darkness some distance ahead of her. Assuming the light was most likely being produced by Tinker Bell, she set her steps in that direction.

Her path led her out of the forest, to a spot she could tell was not far from the coast; even though she couldn't see them, she could hear the waves of the sea as they splashed ashore. The moon and stars cast enough light to show her that the ground ahead sloped upward gently before doubtless falling off to the sea below.

The flickering light was positioned not far from where the slope ended and Alice continued to follow its allure.

As she had surmised, the light led her to Peter Pan. He was standing just a few yards back from the edge of the high cliff. His face was turned up toward the heavens, while Tinker Bell was flitting round about him.

"Hello," Alice said tentatively as she drew closer.

"Oh, hello, Alice," Pan replied, lowering his gaze and smiling at her.

"What are you doing?" she asked.

"Tink and I were just talking," he said.

"Oh." Alice felt like she had probably intruded upon what was meant to be a personal and private moment and felt badly for having done so.

"How rude of me," she said, starting to back away. "I'll leave you alone."

"No—it's quite all right," Pan assured her. "We were just discussing plans to travel together to *Foreverland*."

"What?" Alice was somewhat astonished. "You want to leave already? But you've just finished a harrowing adventure that very nearly got you both *killed*!"

"Exactly," said Tink. "And that's the correct word, all right—'*finished*'." She giggled lightly.

"So now it's time to start a *new* adventure!"

"No disrespect intended—but I fail to see the logic in that," Alice protested. Then the full weight of the plan they had announced struck her.

"Besides...how will you know how to *find* Foreverland?"

"Why, I'll simply follow the *map*," Pan explained.

Alice was confused. "What map?"

"The map that was inside the chest we gave Hook and the queen of course!"

"I don't understand," Alice said, feeling even more confused. "The only thing inside the chest was that sheet of parchment—and it was completely blank.

"I know it was. I saw it myself momentarily when I was sneaking up to snatch up Tink's cage. As the queen said, there wasn't a mark on it!"

"I guess you needed to have the right kind of eyes to see the image on the scroll," Pan said. "The eyes of a child, perhaps." He chuckled again.

"It was clear as day to me!"

"What was?" Alice demanded, growing rather impatient.

"The *map* that was drawn on the parchment," Pan explained. "It showed quite clearly where Foreverland is. And I memorized it."

"So now we mean to go there!" Tink exclaimed gleefully.

With that, Pan began to float up off the ground. When he reached the same height as Tink, the two of them began to drift toward the edge of the coastal cliff, following the natural slope of the land to the point where it fell away.

They really were leaving, Alice realized. And what was to become of *her* now? Would she be left to fend for herself here in Neverland? If not, would she somehow be magically transported back to what awaited her in the Real World?

Neither prospect filled her with any joy.

Even though Peter had been right when he predicted she would have several friends by the time their adventure ended (Lots and lots, in fact, if you counted the entire Indian tribe as well as Tiger Lily. And the little people, the Diminii. And Mister Yeti. And Doctor Philogeneas. And she was sure that, in time, she might even be able to win over a mermaid or two.), that didn't sufficiently balance the impending loss of two of her most cherished.

"I guess this is good-bye, then," she said sadly, waving to the floating pair. She had to fight to hold back tears.

Tinker Bell flitted close to Pan's left ear, chatting away in fairy speak. As she did, the boy's face brightened.

"Tink's just had a *wonderful* idea!" he called back to Alice.

"Why don't you come *with* us to Foreverland?"

"Could I?" Alice asked, her spirits rising at once. "Could I really?"

"Of course; you're more than welcome." Pan waved his arm. "Come on!"

Alice held her arms up and out toward Pan. "Come get me then!" she said eagerly.

"Oh, no," Pan replied, his face showing concern. "It's quite far to

Foreverland—and I'm afraid I couldn't possibly carry you such a long way."

"Then however shall I get there?" Alice practically sobbed.

"You'll just have to fly on your own."

"But I can't. I don't know how!" she wailed.

Even as they spoke, Pan and Tink were rising higher in the air and continuing to drift seaward. Walking briskly, Alice followed behind them, moving rapidly toward the edge of the cliff.

"Of *course* you know how, Alice," Pan admonished lightly. "The first thing you have to do is *believe*—the way only a child truly can.

"You have to totally, completely, one hundred percently—believe!"

All the wondrous things Alice had encountered during her short time in Neverland flashed before her eyes: fairies and mermaids and giants and Yetis.

After having seen all that—how could she *not* believe in something so simple as being able to fly just by wanting it?

Alice now quickened her pace. She began to run after Pan and Tink, totally unmindful of the harsh fact that the land upon which she trod was about to end in a hundred-foot drop to the sea.

"I *do* believe!" she called out to them.

"Then, only one thing else remains," Pan told her. "You have to be *free*. Do you want that?"

"I—I *think* I do," the girl panted.

"Freedom doesn't come from the *head*, Alice—it comes from the *heart*!" Pan's voice was growing slightly fainter as he rose higher into the night sky.

"Be free—and you can fly!"

Alice was running faster and faster in pursuit of the magical pair—and the edge of the perilous cliff was drawing closer and closer.

"Oh, Peter…I can—I can!" she shouted exuberantly, starting to feel the ground fall away from beneath her feet.

"*I can fly!*"

And that's exactly what Alice did.

-THE END-

About our Creators

WRITER –

R. A. JONES - is a native of Oklahoma (originally Indian Territory) where he still resides. R. A. has been a freelance writer and editor for the past thirty years.

His credits include newspaper and magazine columns, articles and short stories. He has been a movie reviewer and commentator in newspapers and on radio. He assisted actor Gary Lockwood (Star Trek; 2001: A Space Odyssey) in the writing of Lockwood's autobiography, *2001 Memories: An Actor's Odyssey*. With Michael Vance, R. A. co-wrote the syndicated comic book and comic strip review column *Suspended Animation* for five years.

The readers of *Comic Buyer's Guide* magazine voted him "Favorite Writer About Comics" in 1985, and in 2006 he was inducted into the Oklahoma Cartoonists Collection Hall of Fame.

He has scripted more than 100 different issues of various comic book titles in his career. Among the more noteworthy are Wolverine and Captain America for Marvel Comics; *Harlan Ellison's Dream Corridor* for Dark Horse Comics; and Star Trek: Deep Space Nine for Malibu Comics. He also co-wrote, for Image Comics, *Bulletproof Monk*, which served as the basis for the 2003 movie of the same title.

His comic book stories, "Cold Hard Facts" and "Three On A Match" which originally appeared in the magazine *Metal Hurlant*, were short films in France.

His novels include *Deathwalker, Global Star* (written with Michael Vance and Mel Fox), *The Equation* (co-written with Michael Vance), *The Steel Ring*, a superhero book based on characters from one of the earliest publishers of comic books, Centaur. He also wrote the Western thriller, *Gun Glory*.

INTERIOR ILLUSTRATOR –

GARY KATO—was born in Honolulu, in 1949. He graduated from the University of Hawaii with a Bachelor in Fine Arts degree. His comic book work has appeared in such varied titles as Destroyer Duck, Thunderbunny, Ms. Tree and Mr. Jigsaw. He's also illustrated children's books such as The

Menehune of Naupaka Village and the currently available Barry Baskerville Returns and Jamie and the Fish-Eyed Goggles. He's also been a contributor to the Children's Television Workshop magazines, 3-2-1 Contact and Kid City.

COVER ARTIST –

TED HAMMOND - is a Canadian artist who has been creating amazing art for over twenty years. His work has appeared in magazines, ads, books and graphic novels just to name a few. Go to (www.tedhammond.com) to contact him and check out more of his work!

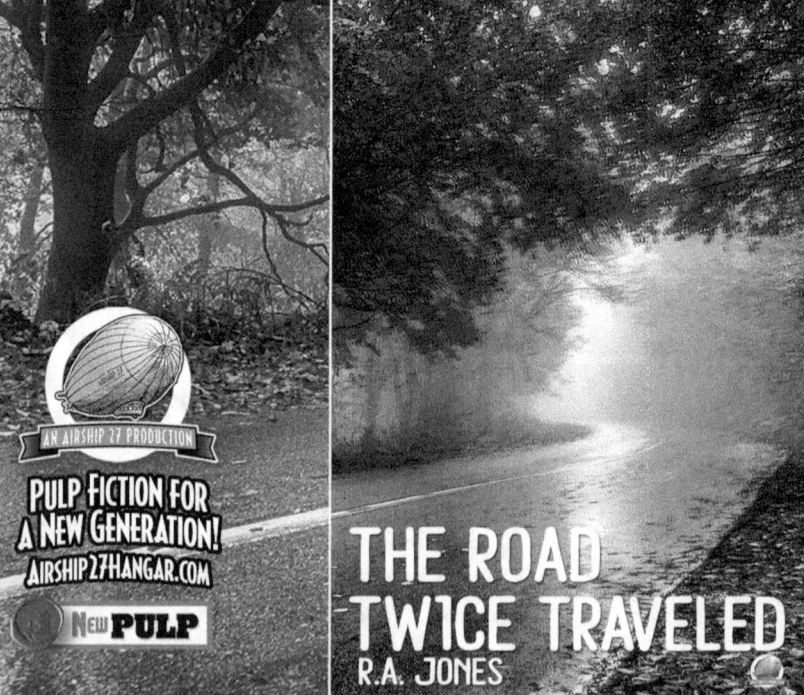

www.ingramcontent.com/pod-product-compliance
Lightning Source LLC
Chambersburg PA
CBHW051131260626
47170CB00005B/1759

* 9 7 8 1 9 4 6 1 8 3 9 3 4 *